The Witcher

THE WITCHER

JOAN WEIR

POLESTAR
BOOK PUBLISHERS

Polestar Book Publishers acknowledges the ongoing support of
The Canada Council for the Arts, the British Columbia Arts Council,
and the Department of Canadian Heritage.

Cover artwork by Ken Campbell, Imagecraft Studio
Cover design by Jim Brennan
Printed and bound in Canada

Canadian Cataloguing in Publication Data
Weir, Joan 1928-
The witcher
ISBN 1-896095-44-5
I. Title.
PS8595.E48W5 1998 jC813'.54 C98-910145-2
PZ7.W44Wi 1998

Library of Congress Card Catalog Number: 98-84381

Polestar Book Publishers
P.O. Box 5238, Station B
Victoria, British Columbia
Canada   V8R 6N4
http://mypage.direct.ca/p/polestar/

In the United States:
Polestar Book Publishers
P.O. Box 468
Custer, WA
USA   98240-0468

5 4 3 2 1

For Christina, Rachelle and Mitchell, who know Raj;
For Courtney Luft, who takes such good care of him;
And for Mackie Pozzobon, who taught me about witching.

To Ian — thank you.

"I wonder why people think twelve is such a great age?" Lion remarked across the dinner table, pushing at the crest of blond hair that, as usual, was falling over his eyes. "It sucks."

"So does having to live with a twelve-year-old brother," Lion's sister Bobbi suggested.

"I might add," Dad put in, frowning, "so does your language."

Lion glanced at Dad from under his eyebrows, so it wouldn't be obvious that he was watching, and waited. It used to be that he could smart-talk Dad anytime and Dad would go along. But lately, since Mom had left, Dad sometimes got mad. However, this frown of Dad's didn't look like a red-alert frown. It looked more like an establishment one to go with the grey suit Dad was still wearing from his day at the office.

"Are we allowed to ask what has prompted that earth-shattering conclusion about age twelve," Dad said at last, "or is it a secret?"

Lion grinned and felt the tension ooze away. Sure, his dad was still scowling, but that's one of the few good things about being twelve. You're so used to being scowled at, you don't even notice anymore. It's when people smile that you start to worry. "No secret. Twelve sucks because if I was fourteen like Bobbi, you wouldn't make me go along on this trip you're planning, and if — "

"Oh, yes I would."

" — and if I was only ten," Lion went on as if his dad hadn't spoken, "I wouldn't mind." He helped himself to a huge mound of mashed potatoes.

"I see. Well, in that case I've got a suggestion," Dad said, slicing the meat loaf.

Eagerly Lion looked up. Actually, he was twelve and a quarter, not just twelve, and now he did his best to look twelve and a half. "You mean I can do a *Home Alone*? Hey, excellent! I'll pig out on cheese pizza and stave off house-breakers while you and Bobbi do the Superman thing and right the wrongs of the world."

"That wasn't my suggestion, though it's tempting," Dad said wryly. "Unfortunately, I'd be arrested, and I'd just as soon not." He watched as Lion added a third huge spoonful of gravy to a plate that was already crowded. "I presume you're planning to spend the evening washing the tablecloth when that mess overflows."

Lion's grin widened. He set to work stirring the potatoes. When the whole mound had dissolved into brown soup he began forking it into his mouth. It oozed through the tines.

"Must you do that?" Bobbi protested. "It's gross."

With his fork in mid-air, Lion paused. He studied the gooey mess. "You're right," he agreed. "It is kind of gross. It needs a tinge of green in with the brown, then it'd be exactly like soft manure."

"Mega gross."

Lion returned his attention to the business at hand. "If I can't stay alone, how about letting me stay with one of the neighbours?"

"I don't imagine they're particularly keen to be arrested either."

This was so unexpected Lion forgot about acting twelve and a half. "Pardon?"

"They'd murder you within twenty-four hours."

Bobbi burst out laughing. "If only they would," she said wistfully.

"Why don't we let him stay with one of them and see?" Dad grinned.

Lion tried a new tack. "Actually, I'm thinking of the future," he said thoughtfully. "It's gonna be a few years yet before Bobbi or I can move out, and it'd be dumb to strain the relationship. Maybe you've never thought about it, but there are two kinds of families. Those who still get all dewy-eyed when they think about family togetherness, and those who have just finished spending their family vacation in a camper."

"We're not going to be living in a camper," Dad replied. "And even if we were, it wouldn't be a problem. We'd take along a wagon and tie you on a rope behind."

Things weren't going well. "So, what was your suggestion?"

"That you accept defeat and pack your stuff."

"Come on, Dad. How do you know they even have running water up in that gold rush country you're going to? Have you given any serious thought to the combination of mosquitoes and outdoor plumbing?"

"You'll just have to learn to be quick."

"What about TV? There probably won't be any. And there isn't a hope there'll be any Nintendo."

"I know you won't believe this, Lion, but trust me. There actually was life before Nintendo."

Lion knew when he was defeated. He reached for the gravy dish and poured another huge spoonful over his potatoes. "So when do we go?"

"Day after tomorrow. We'll start first thing in the morning. It's a nine hour drive and I want to be there by suppertime." Dad paused and looked at Lion from under half lowered lids for a minute, then added, "That will give you and Bobbi all day tomorrow to clean your rooms and hose down the horse trailer."

"The horse trailer! What's the point in hosing down the horse trailer?"

"We're taking it with us."

"With Bobbi's horse?"

Dad nodded.

"Then she can hose it down."

"Your horse will be in it, too."

Obviously Dad was trying to be funny. They only had one horse and that was Bobbi's.

Dad finished his last mouthful of meatloaf and put down his fork. "I'll be busy most of the time while we're up in gold rush country. This will be a way for you two to get around and take in some of the historic sights."

"On one horse?" It was Bobbi who protested this time. Lion was no longer concerned with minor things like horses. He was still reeling from the mention of historical landmarks. It sounded like a category in *Jeopardy*, or *Reach for the Top* — which was reason number four-thousand-and-two for not going.

"Don't worry," Dad told Bobbi. "I don't expect poor Brie to carry both of you. I've bought a new horse for Lion. It's being delivered tomorrow morning."

Stunned silence greeted that remark. Then Bobbi protested, "But Lion hates horses!"

The hint of a smile pulled at the corners of Dad's mouth. "We'll have to hope he changes his mind."

There was no way Lion was getting up on any horse. Dad had to listen to reason!

It was too late. Before Lion could gather his forces, Dad was on his feet. He paused just long enough to hold up the wooden salad fork, point to the mound of green gunk dried between the tines, and ask if Lion and Bobbi might please try a little harder in the dishwashing department before they all died of bubonic plague. Then he left the room and disappeared into his study.

2

"He can't mean it," Lion muttered in a hollow voice as the study door closed.

But it seemed Dad was serious. Shortly after breakfast the next morning, a large horse van pulled off the highway and started down the winding drive.

"It's here," Bobbi announced, pointing through the living-room window. "Let's go see your new horse."

Lion continued reading his Power Ranger comic.

"You're like a three-year-old playing hide and seek," Bobbi told him angrily. "The horse isn't going to go away just because you pretend you can't see it." She headed out the door.

With a sigh Lion tossed down the comic and followed. With luck she could be wrong — maybe there was some way he could make the horse disappear. He'd work on it.

Their house sat on a two-acre lot about twenty kilometres out of the city in the centre of a sleepy suburb. In front was a big fenced field, ankle deep in grass, with a three-sided wooden shelter in the far corner, circled by a corral. When their mom had still lived with them they'd had two horses, but for the last little while it had just been Brie.

The driver stopped his van, lowered a wooden ramp, disappeared back inside the van then reappeared with a horse held on a short lead rope. Slowly he led the animal down the ramp. The horse was a dark bay colour, with a brown mane and tail, white on all four feet and a wide white blaze down the front of his face. Only the blaze wasn't really in the centre. It started that way. Between his eyes, it was exactly where it should have been. But as it moved down the horse's face it shifted to the right, so that by the time it reached his mouth he had one white nostril and one brown one.

"What a dumb-looking horse," Lion said, noting the off-centre blaze. Then he noticed the white feet and he started to grin. "He reminds me of a four-legged basketball player who's fighting a losing battle to keep his socks up."

Bobbi laughed. It was true. Each of the horse's white socks came to a different height.

The horse had been proceeding quietly down the ramp, concentrating on the narrow footing, but at Lion's words his head came up. Lazily he glanced over. For a fraction of a second he seemed to be studying Lion, then he returned his attention to the ramp. Lifting each foot as daintily as if he was walking on expensive carpet instead of potentially slippery wood, he continued his way down.

"Great," Lion muttered. "Just what I needed. A reject from the dog food cannery. He's got about as much get-up-and-go as a turtle."

The horse's ears twitched forward at the words, but this time he didn't look round.

"He heard you," Bobbi remarked dryly.

"Even smart horses don't understand words."

"They understand tone of voice. Anyway, don't be so sure this one's dumb." Bobbi was studying the new horse carefully. "Dad said he was a pretty high-class cutting horse, and that takes lots of brains."

"What's his name. Did Dad say?"

"Rajah. He's a purebred Arabian."

The frown on Lion's face changed to a broad smile. "Then it's not only the horse that's dumb. So is his former owner. A rajah is an Indian prince, not an Arabian one."

"So change it."

Lion shook his head, still grinning. "No way. It'll remind me how dumb he is."

The van driver moved toward where Lion and Bobbi were standing. "You want me to put him through there?" He pointed to a wide iron gate leading into the grassy field where Bobbi's horse Brie was grazing.

"I'll take him," Bobbi said, moving forward.

Without argument, the driver handed over the lead rope and returned to his van. Next minute he'd swung around in the driveway and was heading back toward the main road.

Bobbi continued studying the new horse. "You're wrong. He's not dumb looking," she said at last. "In fact, he's got class. Look at the way he picks up his feet, and holds his tail. I bet he looks really great when he trots."

"If he trots."

"Okay, maybe he is a bit quiet, but you're not exactly Cowboy Clarence. Better to have a horse on the quiet side than one whose whole mission in life is to dump the rider." She moved closer and rubbed behind the horse's ears. Rajah leaned into her hand. "See! He's gonna be fine." She continued to rub. Raj continued to lean.

"Watch it or he'll fall asleep," Lion said dryly.

"You want to try him now, or let him get used to the place first?"

"I don't want to try him ever."

Bobbi ignored that remark. "I think we should let him get used to us first. I'll put him in with Brie. While they get acquainted we can hose down the horse trailer like Dad said." She led Raj through the gate, took off his halter and turned him loose. Raj stood motionless. He gazed all around. He looked back at Bobbi. Then, as if he had all day and nothing to do in it, he started lazily down the field toward where Brie was grazing.

"What beats me is where Dad found him," Lion muttered.

It didn't take long to clean the horse trailer. As soon as that was finished, Bobbi and Lion went back to the house to tidy their rooms. At least, Bobbi tidied. Lion considered the matter. He was still considering when Dad arrived home a little after five that afternoon.

As he walked past the open door of Lion's bedroom, Dad paused. For a long moment, he studied the scene. The bed was unmade — or it probably was. It was hard to be sure through the layer of discarded clothes, comics and CDs. The area immediately in front of the closet resembled a garbage landfill when the city staff are on strike. Sports gear, runners, a tennis racket, even a heavy parka not used since last winter had all been discarded en route, with the result that the closet door couldn't close. On the desk, a pair of pajama bottoms, one runner and three mismatched socks — each with a hole — crowned a rubbish heap of comics, gum wrappers, half-used glue tubes and empty model boxes. The runner's mate was on the chair, together with four crumpled T-shirts, three pairs of dirty jeans, several pairs of undershorts and an army of round woolly sock balls which were the result of socks being pushed off over the toe, half inside out and half right way round.

"Would it be rude of me to ask if this is before or after you've tidied up?" Dad asked.

Lion's gaze followed his dad's. "Actually, I've been having trouble getting started," he admitted. "I keep remembering something you said the other day."

Dad's eyebrows lifted.

"It was just after we'd listened to the news. You were kind of depressed, remember? We'd just been told how the ozone layer was breaking down, how the polar ice caps were melting and how one small computer slip-up somewhere could mean nuclear disaster. You said if people didn't smarten up we were gonna be in big trouble."

"I remember," Dad conceded. "But what's that got to do with cleaning your room?"

Lion moved his arm in a wide, sweeping gesture. "Imagine how I'd feel if I spent hours cleaning this mess the very day before the world ended. I'd never forgive myself."

"See if between now and tomorrow morning you could try," Dad said dryly.

3

Shortly after eight the following morning, Bobbi stood by the back of the station wagon. The horses were loaded in the horse trailer, contentedly munching on a manger of alfalfa hay. Dad was completing his final check of the house. As soon as he was finished they'd be on their way.

"You still don't seem very happy about coming with us," Bobbi said to her brother as she put her suitcase through the open tailgate.

Lion caught the tinge of concern under the words. He wanted to tell her that it wasn't because he didn't want to do things with her. He liked her a lot. In fact, since Mom left Bobbi had sort of filled that awful hole for him. But a guy couldn't come right out and admit a thing like that to his own sister — at least not without feeling really embarrassed. So loading his case into the car beside hers he said airily, "Driving's boring, that's all."

"Great." Without another word Bobbi turned away and climbed into the front passenger seat.

"Are we gonna take turns getting the front?" Lion asked, following her around the car and opening the door of the second seat.

"Not if I can help it."

Lion went funny inside. "Bobbi, I didn't mean —"

"Get lost, okay?"

The feeling got worse. He'd never admitted it to anybody, but ever since Mom left he'd had a gnawing feeling deep inside that maybe he was to blame. Who else was Mom mad at so often? What if after a couple of weeks of vacation to-getherness Bobbi decided she didn't want anything more to do with him either? What if Dad decided he'd had enough too, and took off like Mom had?

Also, there was something else. It wasn't that he didn't want to go with Dad and Bobbi, but he was twelve and a quarter. When somebody twelve and a quarter hangs around with his dad and his big sister it looks as if he doesn't have any friends. He turned so Bobbi couldn't see his face. His sister was altogether too good at guessing what he was thinking. Swiping at the hair that as usual was falling over his eyes, he climbed into the back seat.

A moment later, Dad reappeared in the doorway. "I think that's it," he announced. He pulled the front door closed, checked to make sure the lock had caught, then crossed the lawn and got into the car.

"So tell us more about where we're going and why," Bobbi said, ignoring Lion in the second seat.

For a moment Dad was busy negotiating the turn from the drive onto the freeway, then the car settled into a com-fortable speed and he relaxed. "The answer to 'where' is a little ghost town called Wells which is right in the middle of the old gold rush country. As to 'why,' the Ministry for Children and Families has asked my opinion concerning a custody wrangle. They've had a home study done by their own social workers but the results are inconclusive. They'd like me to give them an independent opinion."

"What kind of custody wrangle?"

"It seems several people all want to adopt a young witcher."

For the first time, Lion felt a tingle of interest, but he took care not to let that show. Instead he said caustically, "I thought witchers were people who rode broomsticks on Hallowe'en, or stood around and didn't get asked to dance at grade seven parties."

Dad laughed, but Bobbi looked disgusted. "Don't they teach you anything at school?"

"There isn't time between the field trips and the in-service days. Teachers aren't so dumb. They know how much nicer school is when the kids are kept out."

"Funny, funny," Bobbi returned.

"I bet you don't know what a witcher is either," Lion challenged.

"I bet I do. Witchers are people who can find things like oil and water and gold and uranium and stuff by the radioactivity in their own bodies. Right Dad?"

"More or less," Dad agreed.

"And one of those guys is going to be your client?" Lion asked.

"Indirectly. I've been asked to give my opinion as to which of the three hopeful guardians should be given custody of what you term 'one of those guys.'"

For a moment Lion digested that thought, then asked, "How?"

"How am I going to determine who should get custody?"

"How do witchers find that neat stuff Bobbi said they could. You know — gold, uranium, water —"

"With what are referred to in the trade as witching rods."

Lion's momentary interest faded. "Come on, Dad."

"I'm serious. They use bent pieces of aluminum with a little pouch attached. You can pick one up in any hardware store. Some witchers use one rod, some use two."

"What do the rods do?" Lion asked carefully, still not quite sure if Dad was putting him on.

"They pull."

Now he was sure. His eyes lifted skyward.

"It's true," Dad insisted. "The witcher holds the rod loosely in his hand and if there's any gold or water in the ground the rod pulls in that direction."

Even Bobbi was looking skeptical. "If that's true, and if people can find things like gold or uranium with a bit of aluminum rod, why aren't more people witchers?"

"They don't have enough electricity."

"The rods?"

"The people. Most people would probably register about three on a body electricity test. A good witcher would score more than twenty."

Lion sank back against the car seat. "You know what I think?" His face was serious and thoughtful.

Dad and Bobbi waited.

"That witchers should be careful not to drag their feet over any heavy carpets in the winter."

To Lion the trip seemed interminable. Four hours to Cache Creek, then lunch, then four more hours to Quesnel, followed by a final hour on a twisty narrow road to Wells. If he hadn't been able to talk Dad into stopping every once in a while so he could take a photograph, he'd never have been able to bear it. He'd just about resigned himself to driving for the rest of his life when he felt the station wagon begin to slow. Next minute Dad pulled off the road into the parking lot of a motel. It was the most woebegone motel Lion had ever imagined.

"I knew we should have stayed home," he said hollowly. "Quick, turn around. The time machine has malfunctioned and we're two hundred years in the past."

Dad grinned. "I have to admit it isn't exactly the Pan Pacific, but it's the best Wells has to offer. I told you this was a ghost town." Unwinding himself from behind the wheel he shook the stiffness of nine hours' driving out of his legs, tried to repair the creases in his trousers, then moved toward the door marked "office." Lion couldn't help thinking that Dad's conservative business suit looked a little out of place against the background of weed-choked yards, unpainted buildings and dirt streets, particularly when Bobbi was in shorts and a halter, and when Lion's own jeans and Blue Jay's T-shirt could have used a laundering.

Lion turned his attention to the one-storey wooden motel. It wasn't only the world's dreariest motel, he decided, it also had to be the world's most unpopular. Out of fifteen units, only two were occupied — number seven in the centre where a big sign reading "Caretaker" sat in the window, and number fifteen on the far end, where a man with a dark mustache was standing by the door of a red Camaro. The man was probably either a tourist or a prospector, Lion decided. The bottoms of his drab olive-green pants had been laced tight inside the tops of heavy hiking boots as if to keep out dirt and insects, and a pair of binoculars was slung around his neck on a cord.

The man had been concentrating on adjusting the strap of his binoculars, but as Dad and Lion and Bobbi climbed out of the car he glanced over and studied them with interest. "Welcome to Wells," he said in a neighbourly tone. For a minute longer he smiled at them, then with a half wave he turned and got into his car. Next second he was wheeling out of the parking lot.

"Too bad people aren't as friendly as that in the city," Bobbi said, staring after the Camaro.

"I'll just check in," Dad said, heading for the motel office. Moments later he re-emerged with a key in his hand. The unit the caretaker had assigned to them was number six, the one next to the office. To Lion's relief, it looked better inside than out. There was a living room, a kitchen, two fairly large bedrooms and one small third room just barely large enough to hold a cot and a dresser.

"Don't tell me, I can guess," he said, taking his bag into the small third room without waiting to be told.

Dad grinned. "Unpack your things then we'll drive the horses to the pasture I've rented. It's a couple of blocks from the motel. While you two get them settled I'll make a couple of business calls, then we'll have supper and head out before dark to meet one of the potential guardians. Her name is Mrs. Goodchild. She's the aunt of the witcher and is the person the child welfare people are favouring."

"Can't the kid and his aunt settle it themselves?" Lion asked, following Dad into the middle bedroom. "Why do they need you?" He half expected Dad to ignore the question or say not to be nosy, for Dad never talked about business with them.

To his surprise, Dad said thoughtfully, "It has to be settled officially by the Ministry. Both Spud's parents died a while back in a fire on their ranch. Mrs. Goodchild is Spud's nearest relative and has filed an application for guardianship rights." He paused to unlock his suitcase. "But as I told you earlier, two other people also want to adopt and have filed applications to have action on Mrs. Goodchild's request halted."

"So you're here to try to get it unhalted?"

Dad smiled. "The law society would probably put it in slightly different words, but yes. That is, if after I talk with her and the other two parties I decide she's the proper person to be Spud's guardian."

"You think she might not be?" Bobbi asked.

"I don't know."

Lion's face had clouded into a frown. "This witcher guy is just a kid?"

"Same age as you."

The frown changed to disbelief. "Isn't anybody committing murder anymore, or embezzling some pensioner's life savings, or knocking off an international bank? Since when does the most successful lawyer in Vancouver start spending his time arranging adoptions?"

"Cheer up," Dad said with a smile, unpacking his suits and extra pants. "There are some interesting twists to this case. Who knows? Before it's done it might even involve some of those things you've just listed."

For the first time, Lion was glad he'd come. "Hey, excellent! I'll help!"

"Are you sure you couldn't just let me muddle through on my own?" Dad said at his driest, his attention once again on his clothes. "I know it will be tough without your help, but

I can't be selfish. Those poor horses need you to exercise them by taking them sightseeing."

Lion grinned. Of course Dad wouldn't let them into anything concerned with business, but that didn't mean a person couldn't do a little sleuthing around on his own. After all, how often did a guy get a chance to mess with neat things like murder and international swindles and grand larceny?

For the past few minutes Dad had been regarding Lion with a puzzled expression. "Is it because you don't trust the motel staff?" he said at last, nodding at the suitcase Lion still held in his hand. "Or is this some modern exercise fad I am not aware of?"

With a start Lion realized that while he'd been busy thinking about swindles and murders, both Dad and Bobbi had unpacked. He grinned and put his suitcase down. "I'll unpack as soon as we get back."

Dad didn't argue. He drove them to the pasture, unhooked the trailer, said for them to walk back to the motel after they had the horses settled, and drove off. Immediately Bobbi moved to the rear door of the horse trailer, unfastened the latch and moved inside.

The trailer was constructed so that the horses were tied side by side facing forward, with a waist-high partition between them. That way, the movement of the trailer wouldn't throw them against each other. There were windows on the sides and across the front, and directly in front of each horse was a deep manger for hay or alfalfa. Over each manger a heavy ring had been fastened securely into the trailer wall. The horses were tied to these rings on shank ropes just long enough to let them move their heads up and down and sideways, and even to back up a step or two, but not long enough for them to get themselves caught or twisted around in the narrow stalls.

As Bobbi opened the trailer door, both horses swung their heads around inquisitively. "Good girl, Brie," Bobbi said, patting the mare on the flank. "I know you're sick of being stuck in this cramped trailer, but we'll have you out into a nice grassy pasture in about two seconds." As she spoke, Bobbi unsnapped the clamp on Brie's shank rope and began edging the horse gently backwards toward the door. There was one moment of hesitation as Brie felt her hind hoofs reach the end of the trailer, but Bobbi spoke to her reassuringly and the next moment Brie had stepped obediently onto the grass.

"Okay, your turn," Bobbi told Lion. "Take him slowly and he'll be fine."

Unenthusiastically, Lion moved into the trailer. Rajah, like Brie, watched inquisitively. Lion moved forward to where the shank rope was attached to the ring. Rajah continued to watch. But just as Lion reached for the clasp to unhook the rope, Rajah must have decided he was hungry. He ducked his head back down into the manger, pulling the rope so taut that there was no slack left for Lion to unclasp it.

"You didn't believe me when I said he was dumb," Lion muttered in a disgusted voice to Bobbi, who was waiting in the doorway. "He doesn't even have the sense to get out of this crummy trailer." He pulled at the bay horse's head trying to lift it up.

The head didn't budge. Rajah continued to eat alfalfa.

Lion pulled harder. This time Rajah obeyed.

"Good. Maybe the dumb animal has finally realized who's boss," Lion muttered, relaxing his hold on the halter and turning to once again undo the shank rope.

Rajah plunged his head back into the hay.

Bobbi burst out laughing. "Here. You keep an eye on Brie. I'll get him." She edged past Lion.

Up came Rajah's head, this time without any pulling. He stood motionless while Bobbi unclasped the shank rope from the bolt at the front of the trailer. Then with one blandly innocent glance toward Lion, he obediently moved backward and stepped down onto the grass without the slightest hesitation.

"That horse isn't stupid," Bobbi said, still grinning. "He's got your number."

In Lion's opinion, that remark didn't even deserve an answer.

"If you two are ready," Dad said, getting up from the restaurant table where they'd had supper, "we'll head out to Mrs. Goodchild's ranch."

Half under his breath Lion ventured a comment that included the words "sick of that dumb car," but no one paid any attention and he didn't push it. More driving was better than being stuck all evening in that dreary motel.

"What do you think of your horse?" Dad asked as they left the town of Wells and pulled out onto the main highway.

"I'm trying not to think of him at all."

"Lion says he's dumb, but he's not," Bobbi put in.

"What's with this cutting horse thing?" Lion asked, leaning forward. "According to Bobbi you said he was something special."

"He is. A good cutting horse can save a rancher thousands of work hours."

"How?"

"When the rancher wants to single out a cow for market or a calf for branding, or to cut out one particular animal from the rest of the herd, he just points the cutting horse at the animal he wants, tells him to hold that animal, and sits back. Next thing you know, the rest of the herd has moved on and that cow or horse or calf is still right there where he's supposed to be."

"Some guy told you Rajah could do that!" Lion's voice was scathing. "You got conned, Dad. That horse isn't even smart enough to back out of a horse trailer so he can eat grass."

He turned his attention to the scene outside the car window. Dad had better hurry if he wanted to get there before dark.

Bobbi was watching Dad closely. "Can I ask a question?"

Dad glanced across the front seat at her and smiled. "What sort of a question?"

"One that probably isn't any of my business," Bobbi admitted. "You said two other people had filed requests trying to halt Mrs. Goodchild's request for guardianship rights to the witcher. What's so special about him? Why do all those people want to adopt him?"

"Because he's a witcher, of course," Lion quipped from the second seat before Dad could answer. He waited for someone to laugh.

To his surprise nobody did. "You mean that's right!"

"I'm afraid it could be a real possibility. The whole area around here, particularly where Mrs. Goodchild has her place, is so dry it's practically desert. A witcher who could find underground sources of well water would be worth more than a winning ticket on the lottery." Dad paused. "But there are two other possible answers. Spud's parents owned a thriving horse ranch. Whoever adopts Spud will step into virtual control of that ranch."

"What's the other possible answer," Bobbi prodded as Dad's attention focused on a particularly narrow hair-pin turn on the gravel road.

For another moment Dad was busy, then in an overly casual tone he replied, "The other factor is that this is gold rush country."

"You mean there's still gold here?" Lion's eyes were shining.

"Not like there used to be. But there could be small off-shoots of veins that might have been missed when the big claims were worked a century ago. Don't forget that back in those days they didn't have the sophisticated equipment we have today. Also —" the casual note was no longer quite so casual — "right now there's a rumour going around about a cache of nuggets that could possibly be hidden away somewhere."

"Gold nuggets! Hidden away ever since gold rush days?"

"Mmmm."

"Hey! Excellent!" Lion tried to lean forward so he would be more in the conversation but the seat belt stopped him. "Could a witcher find something like that?"

"A good one could."

"Is this kid good?"

"People seem to think so."

"No wonder all these people want to adopt him." Lion's face was beaming.

The corners of Dad's mouth twisted into the hint of a smile. "The line-up doesn't go quite as far around the block as you seem to be picturing. It's only three so far. There's the aunt, Mrs. Goodchild, there's the ranch foreman and there's also a friend of the family. I'm hoping to get a chance to meet the family friend tomorrow. He is a mining expert who is doing a survey of this area. He was obviously close to the family — he says he has a signed statement from Spud's parents naming him as guardian in the event of their death."

"You mean, people sit around deciding they might die at any minute, so they write letters arranging who's gonna get their kids?" Lion sounded disgusted. "Gross."

"No, practical."

"If he has that in writing," Bobbi said ignoring Lion's interruption, "why wouldn't that decide it?"

"Ordinarily it would, so long as the letter is authentic. But in this case the man works away from home a lot of the time. He doesn't have a wife or any children, which means Spud would be alone. At this point the Ministry is favouring the aunt, who could provide a stable environment and is a blood relative. After her, their second choice is the ranch foreman who together with his wife could provide not only a stable environment but also a familiar one."

Bobbi was frowning thoughtfully. "If all these people love Spud enough to want to adopt him, they must want what's best for him. Why don't the social workers let Spud choose? Why don't they let him say who he wants to live with and let that settle it?"

For a moment Dad seemed to be debating whether or not to answer, then in a carefully emotionless voice he said, "I guess what's worrying everyone is whether these people are asking for guardianship rights so they can look after Spud, or so Spud can look after them."

With that both Bobbi and Lion spoke at once. "You mean they don't love him at all?" Bobbi exclaimed in a shocked voice, while Lion said eagerly, "You mean they want to adopt him so he can find water for them, or that cache of nuggets?"

"At this point nobody knows the answer to either of your questions. But that's exactly what the Ministry intends to find out."

"I can't believe none of them love him. Not even his aunt." Bobbi was clearly upset by the thought.

"She says she does. Ever since the rumours started about the hidden cache of gold nuggets, she has been insisting the witcher business has nothing to do with her wanting guardianship rights. She claims that Spud is just an amateur witcher and couldn't find anything like hidden gold."

"Do you believe her?"

"Let's say I'm keeping an open mind."

Lion's thoughts were still on the gold. "How much would those nuggets be worth?"

"It depends on their size. There is talk that they could be worth close to three-quarters of a million dollars."

Lion let his breath out in a long slow whistle. Gambling on Dad being too busy with the winding road to notice, he unsnapped his seat belt, leaned forward and folded his arms along the back of the driver's seat. "How d'you mean hidden away? Hidden away ever since gold rush days? On purpose?"

He'd been right about Dad being too busy. Dad didn't even answer for a minute. Then the road straightened out. "Yes, hidden away ever since gold rush days, but no, not on purpose. Initially, that cache was probably hidden away to keep it safe. The prospector who found it may have been afraid some of his not too friendly buddies might try to take it away from him. Or he could have hidden it away because winter was setting in."

"What would winter have to do with it?"

"Everything. Don't forget the gold fields were hundreds of miles from civilization and the only form of transportation for the miners was their own two feet. Once winter started, a person would be crazy to try to walk back down the Cariboo Trail."

"So why didn't the miner just wait till spring and then walk out?"

"Something must have happened."

"Like what?"

"A small cave-in, maybe, right in the spot where the nuggets were hidden so he couldn't find them again. Or he could have died."

"I thought the miners who went north for the gold rush were all young guys."

"Most of them were. But even young guys, as you call them,

need to eat, and can freeze to death in an unheated shack when the temperature drops to forty below."

"Forty below!" Lion's voice no longer held any hint of joking. "Why did people stay?"

"A little thing called dreams. They were convinced if they stayed just a little longer and dug just a little harder they'd make that million dollar strike."

That remark seemed to put an end to any more conversation.

Lion went back to staring through the car window at the scene outside. The country they were driving through had to have come from the same order book as their motel in Wells, he decided. Dad was right about it being practically desert. The countryside was ninety-nine percent rocks and sagebrush, and though the remaining one percent was grass, it wasn't grass like Lion was used to. It wasn't green and it didn't sway as the breeze moved over it. It was a yellow brown and so dry it wouldn't have budged if a hurricane had swept through. You could smell the dryness. If Mrs. Goodchild and her neighbours were raising anything he hoped it was camels.

"How can people even grow enough to eat, here?" he said at last.

"You have to wonder. I guess a lot of them can't. Apparently quite a few have their places up for sale."

"Does Mrs. Goodchild?"

"No. But several of the others do. Unfortunately, buyers are hard to find."

Lion continued to stare at the landscape, which looked even more desolate as the light faded. He didn't blame anybody for trying to adopt a witcher if it meant finding a cache of gold nuggets and moving away from this place.

"I still don't see why you're so worried," he said at last. "So what if all three of these people want to adopt this kid so he can witch out a missed vein or find that lost cache of nuggets. If the kid's smart, he'll lay out the ground rules ahead of time — say he expects his cut or he won't play."

"What if he doesn't find anything and they think he isn't trying hard enough?" Dad countered, spacing the words carefully. "Or what if he does find something and they decide they don't want to cut him in? It's kind of hard to stand up for your rights when you're a kid and they are grown-ups."

That side of things hadn't occurred to Lion.

"Besides," Dad said, his tone suddenly innocent. "There's one small detail I haven't mentioned. Spud isn't a he. She's a girl."

"A girl!" Lion's voice was a mixture of disgust and disbelief. "How can a girl find all that neat stuff?"

Dad and Bobbi exchanged glances across the front seat and burst out laughing. It took Lion a full minute to recover his balance. Then, dismissing the girl witcher, he said brightly, "That's what we can do, Bobbi. While Dad's stuck in meetings we can look for that buried treasure. We'll ask the motel lady where we can get a map of all the old mines in the area and then check them out —"

"Let's get one thing clear," Dad said sternly. He glanced back briefly and Lion saw his face. He was no longer smiling. "You can take the horses and ride out to see the flumes and the sluice boxes, but you are not to go near any deserted mine shafts. They are strictly off limits."

"But if there's a cache of gold nuggets hidden some place worth three-quarters of a million —"

"I don't care if it's worth ten times that much, you aren't looking for it. And do up your seat belt."

Grumpily Lion obeyed. "Then why is it okay for the witcher to go looking —"

"I didn't say it was. But in any case it isn't the same thing. Witchers do their witching above ground. They don't go down any mines. The timbers supporting those old shafts have been in the ground more than a hundred and twenty-five years. Can you imagine what sort of shape they'll be in? They didn't use wood preservative back in those days, you know. And even if they did, after all this time the supporting timbers will be rotted right through. One good jar and the whole shaft could come tumbling in around you. If that happened and if nobody knew you were there —"

Even Lion felt slightly daunted. Bobbi looked positively green.

Several minutes earlier they had turned off the main highway onto a secondary road leading into the hills. For the first few minutes it had seemed passable, but now it became narrower and more winding. Dad stopped even trying to take part in the conversation. He needed his full attention on his driving. "This isn't a road, it's a cow path," Lion complained. "It's only wide enough for one car." His eyes smarted from the dust. Ever since they'd left Wells they'd been driving over shifting gravel. "How can you even see if anything's coming?"

"It's not easy," Dad agreed.

"What are you gonna do if we meet somebody?"

"Hope it's a Volkswagen."

At last the road straightened and started up a long hill. They topped the rise and immediately in front of them was an aluminum gate with a sign reading "Diamond A Ranch: Mrs. B.V. Goodchild." Abandoning his grip on the wheel, Dad relaxed against the seat and let out his breath in a long slow sigh.

A metal cattle guard had been cut into the road immediately beyond the gate. The tires of the station wagon hummed as they drove over it. Now, in the valley below, they could see a cluster of ranch buildings. Bobbi was peering intently out the car window. "The one at the left must be the ranch house," she said. It looked rambling and comfortable with yellow eaves and yellow trim around the windows and a matching yellow picket fence. To the right, and set a little way back, was a barn. It was brown and yellow too. In the distance were what looked like chicken houses and a root cellar. Down the north side was a long row of tall Lombardy poplars providing a windbreak for the whole place.

"Will the witcher be there?"

"I hope so," Dad said.

"Can we meet her?"

"I don't see why not."

"If three people are all trying to adopt her," Bobbi went on, her thoughts still on the earlier conversation, "how is it going to be decided?"

"As I've explained, the social workers have already done their home study, but because that study is inconclusive the Ministry would like an independent study done as well. That's where I come in. After I've met with all three claimants I'll present my findings and recommendations, and the Ministry will announce their decision."

"Right then?"

"Perhaps not immediately. But where a child is concerned they won't delay any longer than necessary."

They'd reached the top of the final slope. The car started down. The next moment they were swinging into the ranch yard.

"Hey, there's someone down by the barn!" Lion said, pointing to slim figure in cowboy boots, jeans and a T-shirt who was standing near the doorway playing with a black and white dog about the size of a border collie. Bobbi followed Lion's gaze, but Dad was too busy negotiating the twisty narrow road to look.

The sound of the car approaching seemed to startle the girl. At the same moment, someone else appeared in the yard — a tall and loose-limbed boy who looked about eighteen. He too was dressed in jeans and cowboy boots. His attention was on the girl. She looked from the approaching car to the teenager, then took a quick step backwards, and disappeared into the barn. The dog ran in after her.

"Maybe that was the witcher," Bobbi said eagerly, peering through the window. "Was it Dad?"

For the first time, Dad looked around. "Where? I didn't see anybody."

"She's gone now. She went into the barn. I think she was scared away by that guy."

"Even if she was, it's none of our business," Lion pointed out.

"You just say that because you hate girls."

"Only girls I know." Lion's voice was innocent. Then, as his sister raised her eyes skyward in disgust, he added, "But it's still none of our business."

They'd reached the ranch house. Dad slowed the car to a stop in front of the kitchen door and a woman came out. She was wearing an old-fashioned dirndl skirt and a drab grey cardigan, and she wore her hair caught at the back of her neck in a bun. She looked as if she had posed for the picture on the front of his *Dungeons and Dragons* game, Lion decided.

Dad turned off the engine and got out. He shook hands, introduced himself, then nodded toward Bobbi and Lion. "This is my daughter Roberta and my son Lionel. I hope you don't mind my having brought them along. They're looking forward to meeting your niece."

For a fraction of a second, Mrs. Goodchild looked uncomfortable. The look was gone so quickly that if Lion hadn't been staring right at her he wouldn't have noticed. "I'm very sorry," Mrs. Goodchild said with a worried frown, "but my niece is not well. As you can imagine, this whole thing has been extremely distressing for her. The doctor has given her something to help her relax and has ordered several days of absolute rest and quiet." She smiled. "I'm afraid she won't be able to talk to you, but I will be happy to answer any questions."

"I quite understand," Dad replied.

"Come in, come in, all of you," Mrs. Goodchild urged, indicating the kitchen door. "My son Riley is down at the barn fussing over a litter of kittens that he thinks the barn cat isn't looking after properly, but he won't be long. As soon as he gets here, I'll have him put on a video for the children to watch while we talk."

At the mention of kittens, Bobbi smiled.

"You'd be surprised now many abandoned dogs and sick birds end up being doctored in my kitchen," Mrs. Goodchild said, returning the smile. "I think Riley would even bring the horse in here in the cold weather if I'd let him." Her smile widened. "Do you enjoy watching westerns? I'll get him to put one on for you. He's quite an authority."

At that, Bobbi looked even more pleased. She did like westerns. But then what could you expect from somebody who liked horses, Lion reflected. At least that explained the identity of the guy who had been in the yard a few minutes ago. He was obviously Mrs. Goodchild's son. But who was the girl? He'd wanted to ask but was afraid of sounding rude. If Mrs. Goodchild had been telling the truth, the girl couldn't have been the witcher. Still, Lion couldn't shake the feeling that Mrs. Goodchild was lying. Could there be some reason why she didn't want Dad talking to her niece?

Lion wished that Dad had seen the girl before she took off into the barn. He had a suspicion that something funny was going on. But he didn't want to know what it was so badly that he would spend the rest of the night making polite conversation. "Is it okay if I stay outside for a while?" he asked.

Again, Mrs. Goodchild seemed vaguely uncomfortable. "I think you'd better come into the house with the rest of us. There's not much point in staying outside when you won't be able to see anything. It's almost dark already." She smiled. "This isn't like the city where there are street lights."

Lion couldn't very well admit that he didn't want to get

stuck listening to a boring legal discussion, or that he hated westerns, so he settled for, "That's okay. I like the dark."

"It's true. Lion does like the dark," Bobbi put in brightly.

Her support was so unexpected that Lion practically gave himself away. Bobbi knew he didn't like the dark at all. In fact, she never missed a chance to tease him about it. He glanced over to see why she had backed up his pretense. Then he was sorry, for Bobbi was making unmistakable nodding motions toward the barn. Obviously she too suspected that the girl in the barn might be the witcher and that Mrs. Goodchild might be lying. And she was expecting him to check it out!

Lion pretended not to notice his sister's nods — he wasn't checking out anything. Pausing just long enough to make sure Dad wasn't going to say he had to go in, he eased out of the too-bright circle of light spilling from the kitchen door and melted into the comfortable hazy greyness. He couldn't believe how easy it was. Maybe secret agent wouldn't be such a bad career after all.

Mrs. Goodchild cast a final look in his direction, then turned and piloted Dad and Bobbi toward the house. "As you know, a tragic fire in their horse barn several weeks ago killed both of Spud's parents." Her voice carried clearly towards Lion in the stillness. "For the first little while, Spud wanted to stay and help nurse some of the injured animals, so the ranch foreman and his wife took care of her. But three days ago I brought her here to stay with me. Her mother was my only sister, and I know she'd want me to look after Spud and bring her up as if …" Mrs. Goodchild's words faded as the kitchen door closed behind her.

Lion breathed a sigh of relief. He'd been afraid Dad might change his mind and say he had to come in after all. Now the only question was how to amuse himself for an hour while Dad and Bobbi and that funny Mrs. Goodchild talked. He looked around. The only thing visible through the shadows was the silent barn. He knew his sister expected him to go down there and find out who that girl was. But even if the girl *was* the witcher, Bobbi had no business getting involved. She was too soft-hearted. He'd told her dozens of times that a person had to look out for himself. Sure, it's tough if other people have problems, but that's their business. Maybe Mrs. Goodchild was lying, and maybe she wasn't. Maybe that girl in the barn was scared, and maybe she wasn't. Either way, it had nothing to do with him or Bobbi.

Except … if he didn't check it out, his sister would be really disappointed. After all, she was always doing stuff for him — especially now that Mom had left. He could do this much for her. Besides, it would be something to do.

He started across the dry yard. To his surprise, his footsteps rang out on the hard-packed ground. He hadn't realized how quiet it was in the country. He also hadn't realized how dark it had become. He glanced back at the ranch house. He wished Mrs. Goodchild had left the kitchen door open so the light would shine out. Not that he was scared or anything. No way.

After all, what was there to be scared of?

In the few minutes since Dad and Bobbi had gone inside the ranch house, the darkness had really taken hold. Now it was even hard to be sure where the barn was. The sooner he got there the better, Lion decided. He walked faster. That was one good thing about this area being so dry and flat. Even in the pitch dark you couldn't trip because there was nothing growing —

"Oooof!"

Lion felt as if he'd been tackled by the entire front line of the Dallas Cowboys. When you fell in the dirt at home, you hardly felt it. Here it was like falling on cement. Gingerly, he felt around until he located the large rock he'd tripped over, then took inventory of his injuries. He expected major fractures, but everything seemed to work. He'd live after all. But he'd walk a bit more slowly, he told himself, getting to his feet. There was nothing chicken about walking a bit more slowly. He reset his sights on the vague barn-like shape in the distance. That's when he discovered there were good things and bad things about walking more slowly. The good thing was that you weren't as likely to trip over rocks. The bad was that you could hear better.

What you could hear was silence.

It was unnerving. Lion thought it was quiet where they lived just outside of Vancouver, but even there the noise of the traffic on the highway never stopped. Nor did dogs barking and trucks braking. One night when he couldn't sleep, he'd felt sorry for himself until he realized from the humming of car tires that half the population must be on night shift. Out here it was different. All he could hear was his heart pounding and his footsteps.

His heart stopped pounding. In fact, it stopped beating altogether because he realized he could hear more than just his heart and his footsteps. He could hear somebody else's footsteps.

Stop being dumb, he told himself firmly. Obviously, it was Bobbi. She must have decided to come out after all. He stopped and waited for her to catch up.

She didn't.

"Bobbi?" he said aloud. For some reason his voice didn't sound like his, so he coughed and tried again. "Bobbi?"

He still didn't sound like himself, and there was still no answer, but at least the footsteps had stopped. Obviously he'd imagined them, he decided. Again he started walking. The other footsteps also started, keeping pace a fraction of a second behind his. By now the sweat was running between Lion's shoulder blades. Maybe it was just an echo, he told himself. Maybe open spaces and dry ground did that. Maybe no one was following him at all. But he didn't intend to wait around to find out. If the choice was between tripping over a rock or being grabbed from behind, he'd take the rock any time. He set off at a run.

He kept running until he reached the ramp going into the barn. Then he paused. Now he knew what sensory deprivation meant. The dark inside the barn made the dark outside look like daylight. Why had he ever thought secret agent would be a good career? Space pilot would be way better. If Bobbi wanted this barn checked out, she could do it herself.

Then again, he was the one outside. If the barn was going to be checked, he was the one who should do it. Besides, he admitted with a grin, if he didn't, he'd never hear the end of Bobbi's chicken-after-dark jokes. He took a small step closer to the inky entrance. Then with a wave of relief it dawned on him that he didn't have to go inside the barn after all. He could check it out — and satisfy his sister — by looking in through the windows. Barns had to have windows. He'd walk around outside. If that witcher kid or anybody else was inside, there'd be a light on.

With that thought, his legs stopped feeling like limp spaghetti. He moved down one side of the barn. Lots of windows, but no lights. He moved around the back end. Bingo! In the centre of the back wall, light showed through a tiny opening. But the window was way above head level. Also, he couldn't get close to it because of a huge bush of some kind. In the dark it was impossible to tell what the bush was, but it sure wasn't any of the ornamental shrubs he was used to. It was prickly and scratchy, and it hurt to brush against it.

Then he had an idea. Taking off his jacket, Lion tied one arm to the end of a big prickly branch on one side of the window, pushed the jacket between the bush and the wall, then tied the other arm to a branch on the other side. Using the jacket as a shield, he eased between the bush and the barn wall until he was directly under the window. Then he jumped.

His finger tips just managed to grab the edge of the window ledge.

Great. Now what? Chinning yourself on a bar at school is bad enough, but at least there you're out in the open and you can wriggle around and bring your knees up to help you. Besides, the bar's in your fists and you've got a decent grip. Here, wriggling was impossible unless he wanted to tear himself to shreds on the thorns all around him. And all he had to grip with was the bottom joints of ten fingers. There was no way he could pull himself up.

Still, he'd better give it a try.

With his arm and shoulder muscles screaming in agony, he inched upward. The hardest part would be getting started, he told himself. But as he continued upward he changed his mind. The hardest part was whatever stage he happened to be at. He was panting as if he'd just run five kilometres, and his arms were shrieking. He was just about to decide he couldn't hold on any longer when his eyes drew level with the sill. Then he forgot about his arms and his breathing.

Lion was looking into the barest, dingiest room he had ever seen, and the girl Bobbi had sent him to find was in it. She was sitting at a table on a battered wooden chair with her back to the window, staring at something. The only other furniture in the room was a metal cot that didn't even have a blanket over the bare mattress. Maybe she was the witcher and maybe she wasn't, but Lion couldn't help feeling sorry for anybody shut in a place like that. The only good thing was that she wasn't alone. The black and white dog was sitting on the floor beside her.

Lion wished he could let go with one hand and rap on the glass so she'd know he was there, but if he let go with one hand he'd fall for sure. He'd just have to hope that in another second either she or the dog would sense that someone was looking and turn around. Then maybe she'd open the window and they could —

His cramped fingers refused to hold on any longer. Before he could do anything about it, he was back on the ground. He'd never be able to make that climb a second time, he realized, trying to rub some feeling back into his numb arms and fingers. But it didn't matter. The important thing now was to get Bobbi.

Collecting his jacket from the bush where he'd tied it, he headed back to the house.

Out of the corner of her eye, Spud caught the hint of movement at the window. Quickly she spun around. Was someone there?

For a moment she thought she must have imagined it. The window looked exactly as it had all along. But the black and white dog had heard something too. He'd risen from his spot on the floor, and now, hackles raised, he was moving toward the window.

"What is it, Dusty?"

Standing on his hind legs to reach the sill, the dog peered out into the darkness. A low rumble started in his throat. Spud felt the familiar panic build once again deep in her middle. She had thought she'd be safe in here — particularly when the door was locked. That's why she liked to come. But if that had been him at the window, then it wasn't safe here after all.

Who was he, this man who spied on her? Sometimes she had the strange feeling that he was familiar — someone she knew. If only she could see his face, but he always kept just out of sight. Could he have guessed what she was planning to do? Is that why he was following her everywhere?

She buried her fingers in the dog's thick coat and hugged him tight. As the ruff on Dusty's neck settled back in place and he twisted around to lick her face, Spud felt better. Even if it had been that man at the window, he must have gone now or Dusty would be still growling.

Reassured, Spud went back over to the table and continued leafing through the pages of the large photograph album in front of her. She turned the pages slowly, staring at each picture in turn. As she did so, the tears threatened to gather behind her eyelids.

But after a few moments she found herself once again thinking about that sound at the window and Dusty's reaction. The light had been on and the window had no curtain. Whoever was outside must have seen her, in which case it might not be safe to stay here after all.

Leaving the album where it was, she got up from the table, called the dog and moved along the wall to where an oval-shaped braid rug was hanging.

The next second, both Spud and the dog had disappeared.

It was quicker going back to the house than leaving it, Lion discovered, because the light from the kitchen window acted as a beacon. He steered for it until he was close, then edged into the bushes. He had to talk to Bobbi without Dad or Mrs. Goodchild knowing he was back. That meant finding the TV room because that's where Bobbi would be — watching the B-grade western Mrs. Goodchild had said Riley would show her. The only way to find the TV room was to check the windows. Carefully he moved around the house.

First he found the kitchen, which was empty. Next to it was a tiny bedroom with a sleeping couch and lots of bookcases. It too was empty at the moment, but someone was obviously sleeping there because a pair of clean jeans and a blouse lay on the bed. Then came the front room. The curtains were partly open and Lion could see Dad and Mrs. Goodchild sitting at opposite ends of the sofa, deep in conversation. On the other side of the living room were two more bedrooms — one looked like Riley's, judging from the clothes scattered about in it, and the other would be Mrs. Goodchild's. Those rooms too were empty. Just one room remained. It was the one Lion had been looking for — the TV room. But in spite of Mrs. Goodchild's promise about the video, the TV wasn't on, and Riley wasn't there. Bobbi was all alone, sitting on the chesterfield and playing with a marmalade-coloured kitten — no doubt another of Riley's strays.

Lion rapped on the glass then signed to his sister to open the window.

For a minute it looked as if Bobbi wasn't going to move, then slowly she got to her feet. Using only one hand so she wouldn't have to put down the kitten, she eased the window open a crack.

"If you're still worried about that girl," Lion whispered, "she's in the barn."

"Is she okay?"

"I guess so — if being stuck in a room with nothing but a broken chair is your idea of okay."

"Stop playing games. Just tell me, is she okay?"

"I'm not playing games. You're the one who wanted me to check on her."

Bobbi had been preparing to push the window closed again, but now she paused. "Are you serious about the room?"

"Yes. She's in a room at the back of the barn and I think she's locked in."

Bobbi disappeared from the window. In a flash, she had settled the kitten comfortably in her chair, slipped out the kitchen door unnoticed by Dad or Mrs. Goodchild, and come around the side of the house. "If you saw her, why didn't you find out what was wrong?"

"I just saw her through a window."

"So, why didn't you find a door and go inside?"

"To get to the room she was in would have meant going the whole way through the barn first, and —" Lion broke off, grateful for the darkness which hid the flush he could feel creeping into his cheeks. "And it was too dark in there," he admitted sheepishly.

For the first time, Bobbi's face relaxed into a smile. "I wonder why I didn't know that without asking."

"That's why I came back for you. It won't be scary with two of us," Lion assured her. "Come on." He set off at a brisk walk across the shadowy ranch yard, this time watching for the rock. But after a few steps he stopped. "Did that Riley guy ever turn up?" he asked.

"Uh-uh."

"I thought he was supposed to put on a video for you."

"So did I."

Again Lion started walking, but his thoughts were no longer on the girl in that back room. They were on Riley. Where was he? Mrs. Goodchild had said he was down in the barn checking the kittens and that he'd be back in a minute. But Bobbi said he hadn't come back. And he couldn't have been somewhere else in the house or Lion would have seen him when he checked the windows.

He must still be out in the yard ... or in the barn!

Those footsteps hadn't been in his imagination. Riley had been following him. Right this minute he was probably hiding somewhere in the shadows, watching.

With that thought, goosebumps ran across Lion's shoulders. Why Riley would be following him Lion didn't know, but obviously he was. And if he was planning to jump on them from behind, Lion preferred to have that happen out in the open where he'd at least have a chance to run.

Bobbi had reached the ramp leading into the barn. "Okay, shall we go in?" she asked.

Lion straightened his shoulders. He was almost twelve and a half, he reminded himself. It was his job to look after his sister, especially now that it was just Dad and Bobbi and him. He didn't want to say anything about Riley because that might scare her, but he had to stop her from going into the barn and perhaps getting hurt. So adopting his most casual tone he said, "We'll be able to see better if we stay outside. Come on around to the back and I'll show you that window where I —"

Bobbi didn't wait to hear any more. She moved past him up the ramp and through the barn doorway.

"Bobbi, wait! It's not safe to go in. We can see everything from that back window —"

She had disappeared into the darkness.

The goosebumps on Lion's shoulders were joined by all their friends and relations. What if Riley was in there? Whatever had happened to that nice old custom of girls being timid and chicken? For her birthday he'd sign up Bobbi for two gift bungee jumps.

But if there was one thing worse than having some guy three times your size leap out at you in the pitch darkness and beat you to a pulp, it was letting your sister know you weren't as brave as she was. Giving one more shake to the goosebumps, which only made them worse, Lion followed Bobbi into the barn.

As he had expected, it was impossible to see anything. Leaving the security of the doorway took a bit of resolve. What if he couldn't find it again? But it was okay, he realized looking backward. The doorway was definitely a lighter black than the inside of the barn. He moved farther inside, then stood motionless, listening for any sound of movement.

To his surprise, he discovered it wasn't completely black inside after all — or else his eyes were adjusting. He could make out vague shapes. There was a sort of central passageway with partitions jutting off it. Obviously stalls for horses. He was pretty sure there weren't any horses in them — it was too quiet and it smelled too musty — but that didn't mean Riley wasn't hiding behind one of those partitions, waiting for them to come close enough —

"Bobbi?" he ventured in a half whisper.

Silence.

Where had she disappeared to? He *should* have warned her about Riley after all, even if it had frightened her. Now she wouldn't know enough to hide from him. He inched down the passage. Then his heart stopped beating as hands closed around his arm. Frantically he struggled to break free.

"Shhh!" whispered a familiar voice by his ear.

"For Pete's sake smarten up!" Lion blustered, in a voice designed to fool his sister into thinking he hadn't been scared at all.

That's when he noticed that she must be as scared as he was, for her hands on his arm were shaking. "Somebody's coming," she whispered close to his ear as footsteps sounded on the ramp.

"Quick! In here," Lion whispered, moving out of the main passageway into one of the stalls and pulling Bobbi with him.

"But —"

"Shhh! I'll explain in a minute."

The footsteps moved closer. Lion waited just long enough to make sure it was the guy he'd seen by the barn when they'd first driven up, then ducked his head and held his breath. He hoped Bobbi would duck her head too. He'd read somewhere that faces show up even in the dark. But he couldn't whisper to tell her this in case Riley heard him.

The footsteps drew level to the stall where they were hiding, moved past and continued down the passageway. A bright shaft of light came beaming at them from the end of the barn. Then, as suddenly as it had come on, the light went off again. Had Riley seen them? Lion braced himself for the thunder of returning footsteps.

Nothing happened.

"There must be a room at the end of the passageway," Bobbi whispered excitedly. "That's where the light came from. It's gone now because whoever went in closed the door, but that must be the room where you saw the girl."

"And that guy who just went in is the one we saw by the barn when we first arrived. Obviously he's Mrs. Goodchild's son, because she said he was down here."

Bobbi's face relaxed into a smile. "Then we don't need to worry anymore." She straightened up. "He's come to help her, too. Come on. Let's go talk to them." She started toward the room.

Lion caught her arm. "When we first saw her in the yard you said you thought she might be the witcher. Do you still think she might be?"

Bobbi's expression narrowed. "I don't know. Is it important?"

Lion nodded. "If she's the witcher, then she's not sick in bed — which means Mrs. Goodchild was lying. Riley might not be exactly thrilled at having us find that out."

For a long moment Bobbi stared at him, her expression a mixture of concern and indecision. "It doesn't matter who she is," she said at last. "If she's locked in, we've got to try to help."

"Not when this isn't our property, and when we don't even know these people. There may be a perfectly good reason why she's locked in. Riley has every right to thump us if we just push our way —" The words ended abruptly as the door at the end of the barn opened and again the light beamed out at them. Ducking back behind the partition, Lion pulled Bobbi with him.

"Shhhh!" he whispered again, pressing his lips close to her ear and hoping just for once she'd postpone the argument until they had the barn to themselves.

In the silence, the sound of the door closing seemed almost like a rifle shot. A key grated in a lock, then footsteps started back down the passageway. They passed within a metre of where Bobbi and Lion were hiding then continued out the door.

Slowly Bobbi got to her feet. "She *is* locked in! I heard the key turning." She looked upset. "Why would he lock her in?" Brushing the dust off her shorts, she started down the passageway. "You can keep on saying it's none of our business if you want to, but I'm going to let her out."

Lion knew it was useless to try to stop his sister once she'd made up her mind. Besides, with Riley safely outside, the barn wasn't scary any longer. "Be careful, okay?" he cautioned, moving after her. "If Riley hears us in here …"

Bobbi had reached the small room at the end of the passageway. Waiting just long enough for Lion to move up beside her, she turned the key that was still sitting in the lock and pulled the door open.

For a moment they were blinded by the light, then their eyes adjusted.

The small box-like room looked drearier from close up than it had from outside. The paneled plywood walls had darkened with age, and the bare wood floor was dirty. To the left stood the narrow cot with the bare mattress Lion had seen from the window. To the right was the oilcloth-covered table and the rickety wooden chair. Only now the chair was empty.

"But she was here just a few minutes ago!" Lion protested in disbelief. "Sitting right at that table! And her dog was with her."

"If this whole thing is a joke —" Bobbi's voice was angry.

"It isn't, honest."

"Then where is she now?"

Lion shook his head. He moved toward the table. In front of the chair where Spud had been sitting lay an open photograph album and a partly eaten apple. "Here's the proof that she was here, and not long ago. Look!" He pointed to the bites in the apple. They were just starting to yellow.

"It doesn't make sense! People can't just suddenly disappear!"

It was true. They couldn't. Lion tried to concentrate. The girl had been here just a few minutes ago because he'd seen her, but where was she now? If she'd left by the door they'd have seen her either as they'd been coming into the barn or as they'd crossed the ranch yard. His trip to fetch Bobbi hadn't been long enough for her to sneak out unobserved. Could she be hiding? He looked around. There wasn't even a closet where a person could hide. As for the window, it was too narrow to climb through and too high off the ground, but just to be sure he moved closer. Not only was it latched from inside, the layer of dirt surrounding the latch hadn't been disturbed for months. That meant she couldn't have gone out that way either. Then how had she got out? Where was she?

A new, scary thought struck Lion. They'd fooled Riley in the barn. He'd walked by without even spotting them. But when he got back to the house and found they weren't there, he'd put two and two together. He'd know they must be in the barn, and he'd be back to get them.

"Bobbi, let's get out of here."

His sister wasn't listening. She was staring at the photo album. It lay open on the table next to the apple. "She *is* the witcher," Bobbi said in a low worried voice. "Here's the proof. Look!" She pointed to two large pictures mounted on facing pages. The first showed a clean-shaven man with red hair smiling down at the girl they'd seen in the yard as they'd driven up. Both the man and the girl held funny metal rods in one hand, shaped like up-side down capital letter L's. The caption underneath the picture read, in carefully drawn letters, "Dad and Me Witching."

"Then Mrs. Goodchild *did* lie to Dad about Spud being too sick to talk to him." Bobbi straightened up and started for the door. "We've got to tell him."

"I thought you wanted to help."

"I do!"

"Well you won't help her by rushing off and telling Dad. We'll be put on such a short leash that we won't even be able to leave the motel."

Bobbi had moved away but now she glanced back. "What are you talking about?"

"I'm talking about what Dad's going to do if we rush out

and tell him his client is lying. He didn't see Spud when we did, remember? He was busy driving. When you asked if the person we saw might have been the witcher he said he hadn't seen anybody. What's he going to think if we rush back now and tell him the girl he didn't see in the first place was locked in this room in the barn looking at her photo album, only again he can't see her because she's disappeared."

Reluctantly, Bobbi smiled. "You're right. It could be a bit hard trying to convince him. We'll just have to get some proof." She moved back to the table.

"And just how do you figure we can get proof?"

Lion might as well have saved his breath, for Bobbi paid no attention. She was again studying the album. "Look, here's Riley." She pointed. The picture opposite the one of Spud and her dad witching showed four people: the redheaded girl, the teenager they'd seen in the yard when they arrived, a woman who was unmistakably Mrs. Goodchild, and another slim, smiling woman who had her arm around the girl. The caption under this picture read "Aunt Beverley, Riley, me and Mom."

Bobbi was studying Riley. "Maybe we're wrong about Spud being scared of him. He doesn't look scary here."

"That's because he's smiling."

"No, it's more than that. He looks nice."

Lion wanted to point out that people who lock other people in barns and stalk harmless visitors across deserted ranch yards aren't nice, even if they do smile for photographers. He settled for saying, "Come on, Bobbi. Let's go."

Again his sister ignored him and turned the page.

The next group of pictures had been taken at some kind of family party. The same people were in all of them — the redheaded girl, the redheaded man, the slim smiling woman, Mrs. Goodchild, Riley and a man with a mustache wearing a dark business suit. He was identified under the pictures merely as "Otto." The black and white dog was in some of the pictures too.

Lion had had enough. "If you want to stay here snooping around until Riley comes back and finds you, go ahead, but count me out." He turned toward the door. "And it won't be just Riley who's ticked. Dad will blow his stack if he finds out we're messing around."

"In a minute," Bobbi said absently. She had finished with the album and was now studying the room with a puzzled expression. "This is weird, Lion." She nodded toward the far wall. "The only attractive thing in the whole room is that oval braid rug, so why don't they put it out on the floor where people could see it? Why hang it on the wall behind that table?"

"Maybe they're afraid it will get dirty on the floor," Lion retorted. "Come on. Let's go back to the house to see if the dungeons and dragons lady will give us something to eat."

Several times during the drive back to the motel Lion started to say something to Dad about what had happened. Not only about Mrs. Goodchild lying about Spud being sick, but also about the little games Riley had played.

When Lion and Bobbi had arrived back from the barn, Riley had been sitting waiting for them in the TV room complete with the promised video, a big innocent smile and an absence of explanation. Lion hadn't wanted to make an issue about things right then, but he wanted Dad to know what had happened. He promised himself he'd say something on the drive back. But each time he started to speak, he checked himself. He knew what Dad would say — that Lion was to stay right out of his official legal business. In fact, Dad might make sure he stayed out by grounding him in that dingy motel for the rest of their visit. Nobody else's troubles were worth fixing if that was the price. It was better to put the witcher, Riley and everything to do with the case right out of his mind, he decided.

But his sister had other ideas. The next morning, as soon as Dad's car pulled away from the motel parking lot, Bobbi came looking for Lion. He was in the kitchen in jeans and cowboy boots, demolishing a huge bowl of cereal.

"You want to ride out to Mrs. Goodchild's ranch?" she asked casually.

"Not particularly." The words were thick with granola.

Bobbi tried a new tack. "There's nothing to do around this dull motel. And it would give you a chance to try out that new horse."

Lion took another huge mouthful. "That's even farther down on my favourite activities wishlist."

Bobbi abandoned subtlety. "Please, Lion? You know as well as I do that something funny is going on out at the ranch. We've got to find out what it is and tell Dad."

"Come on, Bobbi. You know what Dad will say if we poke into his business."

"But the witcher needs help."

"We don't know that for sure." Lion finished the last mouthful of cereal, reached for the box and refilled his bowl.

"Of course. How stupid of me." Bobbi's voice was acid. "We won't know for sure that she needs help until she hangs out a large sign with HELP WANTED written on it, will we? Well, do what you want. I'm going out there." She turned away. "Have a good day."

Lion stopped eating. "Are you serious?"

"About having a good day?"

"About riding out there."

"What do you care, since you aren't coming." Grabbing her hat from the coat rack, Bobbi started for the door.

"Okay, okay, I'll come. Only let me finish my breakfast." Four big spoonfuls finished the bowl. He carried it to the sink. His face brightened. "I'll take my camera."

Bobbi had relaxed when Lion agreed to join her, but now she groaned. "No way. You made Dad and me stop at practically every tree all the way from Vancouver so you could take some stupid picture. You've taken enough."

"If I'd had my camera last night when I'd been looking in that room —"

"Good thinking. You could have hung onto that window ledge with your teeth so your hands would be free."

Lion grinned. "This time I'll stand on your shoulders."

It was Bobbi's turn to be serious. "It's not the time it will take," she said thoughtfully. "It's all the stuff you take with you — your tripod and your flash stuff. Rajah could freak out with all that junk tied to his saddle."

"That horse is too laid back even to notice. My worry is whether he can walk that far."

While Lion packed his photography bag, Bobbi chopped some carrots and apples as a treat for the horses. Then they set out on foot for the pasture. As they neared the fence, Bobbi whistled. Brie's head came up and she trotted eagerly toward the gate, leaving Rajah busily munching grass in the far corner of the field.

"Try calling your horse," Bobbi suggested, feeding Brie some of the apples and carrots. "Maybe he'll come too."

Lion whistled.

Rajah continued munching grass in the far corner of the field.

"Try his name. Maybe he's trained to come to that."

Did Lion ever feel dumb. People didn't call horses out of fields. But if the stupid animal would come, then Lion wouldn't have to trudge all that way to get him. "Rajah!" he called sharply. "Come!"

"Not like that, dummy. That's the way you call a dog. Call him like this. Raaaaajahhhhh! Come on boy! Raaaaajahhhh!"

To Lion's amazement, the big bay gelding's head came up and he moved slowly toward them. You couldn't call it enthusiasm, exactly, but he was definitely moving. "How about that! The dumb horse actually knows his name."

"Now you try."

"Raaaajahhh! Here Rajah!" Lion imitated Bobbi's tone.

Rajah stopped moving.

"Come on, dummy!" Lion shouted with disgust. "Don't stop now!"

Rajah's head went back down into the grass.

Bobbi doubled up with laughter. "I warned you yesterday you'd hurt his feelings if you called him stupid."

"Horses don't understand English."

"Then you explain it." Bobbi's voice was still unsteady.

"So, what do I do now?"

"Take him some oats as a peace offering."

"You mean I've gotta walk all that way?"

Bobbi's grin widened. "You'll live."

They had brought two sacks of mixed grain with them in the trailer. Following Bobbi's directions, Lion half filled a two-litre jug. "It'd serve him right if I pretended I was gonna give him this," he said, "then as soon as he was close enough to grab, pulled it away again."

"Good thinking. And how do you plan to catch him tomorrow?"

Muttering darkly, Lion emptied the oats from the litre jug into a pail large enough for Rajah's head, and set off across the pasture.

At the sight of the oats, Rajah sacrificed one-upmanship

to greed and trotted up obediently. Lion had to give him full marks, because having demolished the treat he played fair. Instead of ducking away, he allowed Lion to slip a halter over his head and lead him back to where they'd parked the trailer with its tack box and saddles.

"Now, let's see how he goes," Bobbi said as Lion finished grooming and saddling him.

Obviously the horse had finally realized who was boss, Lion decided, so it was time to exercise a little authority. A running mount should do it, like the cowboys did on TV. He still remembered enough of the fundamentals from when Mom had lived with them and he'd sometimes ridden her horse. Putting both hands around the horn of the big stock saddle Dad had got for him, he shouted, "Haw — let's go!" and prepared to leap up into the stirrup as the horse darted forward.

Only Rajah didn't dart forward. The only thing that moved was his head as he looked back at Lion with a sympathetic expression.

Lion tried again, this time slapping the reins against the horse's neck as he yelled. The sympathetic look changed to boredom.

Bobbi dissolved into laughter. "Stop trying to be John Wayne. Get on him properly, then give him a good kick with your heels."

Muttering darkly again, Lion obeyed. He settled himself in the saddle, rammed his feet hard into the stirrups and grabbed the reins in his fist. Then, determined this time to prove once and for all who was in charge, he kicked with all his might. Rajah took off at a gallop.

For a minute Lion was so amazed the horse could move at all, let alone gallop, that he did nothing but hang on. Then he began considering his options. Number one was to keep going in the direction they were headed, which was directly toward the fence at the far end of pasture. It was five feet high. He'd never been on a horse that had jumped even a five inch fence. That led to option number two, which was to bail out. The only disadvantage to this was hitting the cement-like ground at fifty kilometres an hour.

As the fence came steadily nearer, the idea of bailing out became more and more attractive. He was just making his final preparations when Rajah changed course and moved into a sweeping U-turn. Next minute they were coming back down the field, still at a gallop. Miraculously, a third option had materialized. This option too had a down side, for galloping back would take them to the top end of the field which was also bordered by a five foot fence, but at least this fence had a gate in it — a nice eight-foot-wide gate big enough for a large truck to drive through — and Bobbi was standing right beside it.

"Open the gate!" Lion yelled over the sound of galloping hoofs.

Bobbi jumped to obey.

But Raj wasn't aimed toward the opening. He was heading toward a spot in the fence at least twenty metres to the left of the open gate.

"He doesn't see it!" Bobbi shouted. "You've got to neck-rein him! You've got to make him turn!"

Fear must have sparked Lion's memory, for out of nowhere he remembered what cowboys on television always did. Cutting the reins hard across the left side of the big horse's neck, he pushed his left heel tight into Rajah's flanks. Miraculously, the horse did what he was supposed to and turned away from the pressure of heel and rein. Little by little he started edging over. At last he was in a direct line with the open gate.

"Talk about dumb," Lion said with disgust. "I can't believe you haven't even got the sense to use an opening when it's made for you." Never mind, they were headed for it now. Once through the open gate he'd just sit back and let Rajah gallop until he'd tired himself out and was ready to stop.

They were a dozen strides away from the top of the pasture. Lion could see his sister watching. He knew she hadn't thought he could do it. Well, here was his chance to show off. As they galloped through the open gate, past where she was standing, he'd turn in the saddle and bow.

Eight more paces — five more — two —

Grinning widely, Lion rose in the stirrups and executed a sweeping bow.

The effect wasn't quite what he'd intended. As they drew level with Bobbi mid-way through the open gate, Raj planted both front feet out ahead of him and slid to a halt.

Lion, in mid-bow, carried on alone.

For a moment it was like a freeze on TV, then Bobbi started toward him.

Lion struggled to his feet. "Stupid horse," he muttered, dusting himself off.

"At least that answers the question of whether or not he can walk far enough to carry you out to the ranch," Bobbi said, trying to stop laughing.

She saddled Brie, then helped Lion tie his camera equipment on the back of his stock saddle. Rajah eyed it darkly. "I think he'll be okay," Bobbi said, watching the big bay carefully. "Only make sure you tie everything down firmly so nothing can bang. It's the noise that will frighten him."

Lion nodded, but his thoughts weren't on his camera equipment. It had occurred to him that going to the ranch and talking to the witcher in broad daylight was almost sure to involve running into Riley. "Unless we luck out and Spud's out in the hills witching," he added, telling Bobbi what he was thinking.

"I think you're wrong about Riley," Bobbi said thoughtfully. "I bet he's not the one she's scared of at all. He's not the scary type."

Lion didn't intend to argue, but he didn't agree. Bobbi hadn't been followed across the ranch yard last night in the dark the way he had.

Slowly Spud moved through the bright morning sunlight, her witching rod held out carefully in front of her. She pretended to be concentrating on the dry barren ground, but her thoughts were on the man in the distance. He'd watched her all day yesterday and the day before. And she was almost positive it had been him at the barn window last night.

She was scared.

At first she'd tried to convince herself that he was just curious. Dad used to tell her people often stared at him when he was witching, but he just ignored them. Witchers had to ignore things like that, Dad had always said. If they didn't concentrate, they couldn't witch.

But Spud was sure this wasn't just curiosity. Curious people didn't hang around watching all day from a distance. They came close enough to ask questions — to see what was really going on. They didn't hover just out of sight. They didn't come back in the dark and peer through windows —

Again she glanced around.

Both yesterday and the day before, she'd been annoyed when Aunt Bea had insisted that Riley must go with her if she wanted to witch. She knew she'd never be able to fix things for Dad if Riley's orders were to always keep her in sight. Besides, she wanted to surprise everyone. She'd been trying frantically to think of some way to leave the house without him, and just this morning her chance had come at last. Aunt Bea and Riley had told her they had to go into town for a few minutes on an errand, but that they'd be back by the time she was finished breakfast. Spud hadn't waited for breakfast. As soon as her aunt and her cousin were gone, she had slipped out. Now she was beginning to wish she hadn't. She wished she'd waited until they'd come back from town and Riley had come with her after all, because that man was up on the hillside, watching her again.

Today, for the first time, the man wasn't trying to stay hidden. Today he was making sure she knew he was there — maybe to scare her because he knew Riley wasn't looking out for her. Goosebumps rippled across her shoulders. If he was the person at the barn window last night, was that why he hadn't stayed — because he'd seen Riley in the yard? What did he want? Why was he following …

Unexpectedly, the witching rod pulled sharply in Spud's hand. The man was forgotten. With a start, Spud realized she'd been so busy worrying about the person watching her on the hillside that she'd covered almost fifty yards without once thinking about what she was doing. How disgusted Dad would be. "Concentrate, honey. You've got to concentrate!" She could almost hear him saying it. Pushing everything else out of her mind, she retraced her steps and started again.

The concentration worked. Her fear was forgotten as she thought about Dad. It was as if he was witching right there beside her — as if he wasn't gone after all. Somehow, she promised silently, she'd finish the job he had started. She remembered how upset he'd been in the spring, when he'd first discovered what was going on. She could still remember his words to Mom when he'd told her what he suspected. He'd sent warnings to the people concerned, but they'd ignored him. So he'd decided to come out here in person and set things right. "Because only a witcher can do it," he'd told Mom. Spud's mom had agreed that it was up to him to do something and that he should come out here and try, but just a few days before he was planning to leave, their barn had caught fire. After that, her parents were gone and her life was completely changed.

Spud pushed down the smothering wave of loneliness that threatened to wash over her and continued to move slowly over the dry soil, her witching rod swinging just clear of the ground ahead of her. She would finish the job Dad had started, she promised herself firmly. He'd said only a witcher could do it, and she was a witcher. She'd set things right, the way Dad had planned to. And maybe, wherever Mom and Dad were now, they'd know about it and it would make them happy.

Again Spud glanced around at the encircling hills, this time not to check on the man watching her but to pinpoint exactly where she'd been walking when she'd felt that sudden pull on her witching rod. It had been the first sign that she might be getting close to what she was looking for. What luck that she hadn't ruined everything and given away that the rod had pulled in her hand a few minutes ago. If she hadn't been so busy thinking about Dad, she'd have reacted, and then the man in the hills would have known what it meant. And if that had happened, everything would have been ruined …

Concentrate, she told herself firmly. Slowly, she went over in her mind how Dad had taught her to narrow down a search area. She followed his directions, reminding herself with each step not to let on if her witching rod reacted. She mustn't let the man watching her suspect that she might be getting close.

By mid-morning Lion and Bobbi had left the town of Wells and moved into the hills. With every step, Lion regretted that he'd let his sister talk him into coming. For one thing, the heat was becoming unbearable. It had to be close to thirty-five degrees Celsius, and there wasn't a tree in sight to offer shade. Besides, this wasn't their business. If Dad found out what they were up to, he'd kill them — at least, he would if Riley didn't kill them first. To make matters worse, it was going to take forever to get where they were going because the horses could manage nothing faster than a walk over ground covered with rocks, cactus and scrubby sagebrush.

He was just about to tell Bobbi that she could do as she liked but he was turning back when the path they were following started to climb. As they moved away from the valley floor, the baking heat lessened and there weren't so many rocks and clumps of sage brush to fight through.

"I think we can trot along here," Bobbi said, moving Brie forward as she spoke.

He'd keep going for one more hill, Lion told himself. Then, if the ranch was nowhere in sight, he was turning back. He touched his heels to Rajah's flanks — but gently, remembering what had happened at the pasture. At this pressure, the bay gelding moved obediently into a trot. Head up, ears forward, tail flowing gracefully behind him, he gave the appearance of a well-trained show horse who had never in his life thought of disobeying.

"Didn't I tell you he was well trained?" Bobbi said with approval.

Lion wasn't fooled. He sat rigidly at attention, knee grip tight, hands firm on the reins, alert for any sudden movement.

"Relax," Bobbi told him.

"No way."

"He's not going to run away with you here. Not on this trail."

"Then he'll think of something else."

"What, for instance?"

"He'll put the brakes on again."

"So let him. It doesn't matter if you're only trotting. There's no way you can come off at a trot."

"Don't bet on it." But Bobbi's words were reassuring, and as Rajah continued to be the model of good behaviour, Lion gradually allowed himself to relax. His grasp on the rein slackened. He slouched into a more comfortable position, and because his legs were tired he relaxed their grip against the saddle leathers. He even took his feet out of the stirrups.

"Don't get too carried away, Cowboy Clarence," Bobbi warned. "When I said relax, I didn't mean give up on your knee grip."

"I've realized I don't need a knee grip on this dumb horse. He's finally decided who's boss."

Almost as soon as the words were out, Brie shied at something and leapt sideways. Immediately Rajah imitated her. Lion wasn't sure where Bobbi had ended up but he and Rajah were no longer on the path. They were standing in a clump of prickly sage bushes.

"Ow! Watch out!" Lion clutched his elbows tight against his sides to keep his bare arms from being scratched. "You did that on purpose."

Bobbi was examining the trail. "Don't yell at him, thank him." She pointed to a slowly slithering body in the dirt directly opposite the sagebrush where Raj was standing. "That's what the horses were afraid of. It's only a garter snake, but they didn't know that."

"You mean these horses imagine there are cobras and pythons on the hills outside Wells? That proves how dumb they are."

"Try rattlesnakes."

Lion's grin faded. "Are you serious?"

"Absolutely."

He looked back at the snake. Sheepishly, he gave Rajah a quick pat. "Okay. So thanks, you dumb horse." He returned his attention to the climb. Only another hundred yards or so and they'd be at the top of the ridge. And for the last bit of that distance, he reminded himself, wiping the sweat from his face, they'd be sheltered from the sun because the trail led through a thick shady grove of poplars. It was the only clump of trees they'd seen all morning, and in Lion's opinion it couldn't have been growing in a better spot. But that didn't change his decision to turn around if the Diamond A wasn't on the other side of the ridge, he told himself.

They left the shade of the poplars, climbed the final fifty metres and topped the ridge. Then Lion forgot his threat. The ranch wasn't in sight, but the witcher was. On the sun-baked valley floor was a figure in jeans and cowboy boots, with a baseball cap perched on her carrot-red hair. She was making her way carefully, one hand holding what looked to Lion like a large upside-down capital letter L. A small pouch was attached to the horizontal arm. Every few steps she paused to search the hills behind her.

"There *is* something wrong!" Bobbi exclaimed. "I'm going down to talk to her." As she spoke she touched her heels to Brie's flanks and started down the slope.

"Bobbi, wait!" Lion had dismounted and was pulling at the thongs which tied his camera equipment to the back of the saddle. Scared or not, how many witchers got their picture taken while they were working? "First let me take a picture."

"Who cares about your picture —"

"It'll just take a minute." Lion worked frantically at the knots. He wished Bobbi hadn't made him tie them so tight. "One picture, then you can talk to her as long as you want. Besides," he added, hitting on the argument he knew would convince his sister, "a picture will be the proof you need to convince Dad that something's wrong. After all, if Spud is well enough to come witching, why did Mrs. Goodchild pretend that she was too sick to talk to anyone?"

It worked. Bobbi stopped objecting. Swinging Brie around she came back to where Lion was standing, a short distance down from the top of the ridge. "All right. Only hurry."

Lion went back to his camera. He had taken all his equipment off his saddle and laid things on the ground. Now he started assembling the tripod.

"Do you have to use that?" Bobbi objected. "It would be much faster if you just held the camera in your hand."

Lion didn't even glance up. "Nothing will show from this distance unless I use a time exposure. But I won't be long."

Bobbi's mind had swung back to what Lion had said a moment earlier. "Why would Mrs. Goodchild tell Dad that Spud was sick if she isn't?"

"I guess so Dad couldn't talk to her."

"But why?"

"You heard him say he was to make the recommendation to the child welfare people about who should be given the legal right to adopt her." Lion finally had the tripod assembled. Now he took the camera out of its case, set it on the tripod and turned his attention to the viewfinder. "Maybe Mrs. Dungeons and Dragons is afraid that if Spud gets a chance to talk to Dad, she'll tell him she doesn't want to be adopted by her aunt."

"Maybe." Bobbi was growing more and more uneasy. "Lion, hurry," she said again.

"One more minute." He focused on the small figure down in the valley and began to estimate the light and distance settings. At that moment, the shaggy black and white dog moved into his field of vision. It had come out from behind a large clump of sagebrush where it had probably been looking for field mice, Lion decided, and circled back to the girl, tail wagging. Dropping her witching rod, Spud bent and hugged the dog tightly — in fact, for a minute it seemed to Lion she wasn't ever going to let go. The dog must have thought so too. He squirmed around and licked her face, making her smile. Releasing the dog, Spud picked up the rod and again began witching. But, like before, she stopped every few steps to take a quick searching glance behind her.

Lion felt funny inside. Maybe Bobbi was right. Even if it did mean getting grounded, maybe they should try to do something. The witcher looked as if she really might need help. He knew how he'd felt when Mom had first left. How much worse must it be for the witcher, losing both her mom and her dad —

"Come on, Lion! Hurry up! I want to go down and talk to her."

"Okay, I'm ready." Lion set the time exposure and pressed the shutter release. "Now just five seconds and we can —"

Lion's words broke off abruptly as the bark of a rifle sounded behind them. At the same moment, something ricocheted off the hard ground about twenty metres away.

Bobbi had dismounted at the same time as Lion, but had stayed near the horses, a hand on each set of reins. As the rifle shot shattered the silence, she instinctively tightened her grip. Both horses jumped backward, but, unable to move more than a rein-length, they soon settled down.

In the meantime, Lion had spun around. "Hey! Watch out, eh?" he called, peering back over the ridge. "You just about hit us!"

For a moment he thought he saw movement in that large

clump of poplar trees just fifty metres or so down from where they were standing, and he waited for the person with the gun to reappear. He'd only seen a vague shadow, but one thing was certain — whoever it was had to be pretty dense to shoot without first checking to make sure nobody was close by. Besides, what had the person been firing at? Then he remembered what Bobbi had said about rattlesnakes. Maybe that's what the sharpshooter had been after, but that was still no reason to shoot blind.

"So smarten up, okay?" he called again.

Silence and stillness greeted his words. The person who had shot the gun must have realized how close he'd come to hitting them and had visions of being sued. Either he was still in the poplar grove hiding, or he'd taken off back down the hill.

Dumb nut. But at least that took care of those old fashioned fantasies about how much friendlier people were in the country. Lion turned back to check that Spud was all right.

Once again goosebumps prickled across his shoulders. It was last night all over again. Despite the fact that there wasn't a tree or a hill or even a large rock to hide behind anywhere near the spot where Spud had been witching, the witcher and her dog had both disappeared.

12

For a long moment, Lion's gaze continued to roam back and forth across the valley as he searched for any sign of movement. This business of people disappearing was making him uncomfortable. Where could Spud and her dog have gone?

"D'you think that shot was meant for us?" Bobbi asked, her voice shaking.

"How could it have been? We weren't doing anything. It must have been somebody out target shooting who didn't realize we were here."

But as Lion continued to study the silent hillside a new thought occurred to him. Maybe that shot had been one more attempt by Riley and Mrs. Goodchild to scare them away.

"Don't ignore the obvious," Dad was always telling them when he or Bobbi were trying to make a decision about something. "Most of the time all the facts are there, only people don't take the time to look at them."

Well, the facts this time were clear. Ever since yesterday, Mrs. Goodchild and Riley had been doing their best to keep everyone from talking to Spud. First it was Mrs. Goodchild telling Dad he couldn't speak to Spud because she was too sick. Then it was Riley's turn to follow Lion across the ranch yard and practically scare him to death. When Lion had returned to the barn with Bobbi, Riley had followed them and was probably intending to scare them even more, only he discovered Spud had escaped and had headed off to find her instead. This morning, Riley must have been watching when the witcher came out into the hills. He must have seen Lion and Bobbi following, and decided he'd scare them away for good. So he'd fired that shot.

But that was probably craziness, Lion told himself firmly. Maybe he should take up writing for TV, because it wasn't logic he was using, it was wild imagination. There was really nothing sinister about that shot. It had obviously been fired by somebody out target shooting.

Bobbi had climbed back into the saddle. "Pack up your stuff, Lion, okay?" she told him. "I think we should get out of here."

Lion nodded. Just because he'd convinced himself the shot had been an accident didn't mean he was keen on staying around any longer than necessary. He took his camera off the tripod. He fiddled with the film release, took out the film and tucked it into the pouch on his saddle. Then he put a new film into the camera and set to work disconnecting the sections of his tripod. The routine actions with his camera equipment settled Lion's goosebumps. He began thinking more clearly. He was still uneasy over the disappearance of the witcher and her dog, but there was no way that shot could have been deliberate. It had been some careless hunter who'd shot without looking and now had taken off to avoid getting into trouble. As he fitted the sections of his tripod into their case he told Bobbi what he was thinking.

"Then why can't we see him?"

"Pardon?"

"Look for yourself." Bobbi made a sweeping gesture with her arm.

From where they were standing they had a perfect view of the hillside in every direction. The only cover was that one thick clump of poplars that they'd ridden through on their way up. If the sharpshooter had taken off and was on his way back to Wells they'd have been able to see him moving down that long unprotected length of hillside beyond the poplars. Which meant he couldn't have taken off. He had to be in that clump of poplars — *with his rifle*.

The goosebumps came back.

Bobbi had waited as long as she could. "If you want to take all day to pack that equipment, you can catch up to me," she said, turning Brie and starting back down the trail.

"Bobbi, wait! I've just realized where the shooter must —"

Either she didn't hear over the noise of Brie's iron shoes on the pebbles, or she pretended she didn't.

"Bobbi! Come back!" Lion called again.

She didn't even glance backward.

Lion's throat went dry and his hands started to sweat. Packing his equipment properly was no longer an issue. The only path back down the hillside led right through that clump of poplars. He had to catch Bobbi before she got there.

Making one big lump of his camera and everything else, he shoved it into his photography case, slung the bag over his shoulder and ran for Raj. Untying the rein from the bush where Bobbi had secured him, he prepared to climb into the saddle. But he'd forgotten what Bobbi had said about noisy equipment spooking his horse. Ever since Brie had taken off down the trail, Rajah had been fidgeting nervously, wondering why they weren't going too. Now, as the bulky, clinking camera bag swung threateningly close to his head, the fidgeting turned into crow-hops.

"Dumb horse! Stand still!" Lion thundered.

To his amazement, Rajah obeyed. "It'd serve you right if next time I have a whole hive of mad hornets in here," Lion grumbled as he clambered awkwardly aboard.

Rajah was moving even before Lion had both feet into the stirrups. The spots that had been rubbed raw on the long ride out protested anew as Lion settled back against the hard leather, but he ignored them. Somehow he had to get close enough to Bobbi to call to her, but Brie was running too quickly, her iron shoes sending up sparks as they struck the pebbles on the path. Lion watched in horror as his sister reached the final open stretch leading directly into the clump of poplars. He held his breath. For a moment, he hoped Bobbi had worked out for herself that the sharpshooter must be still hiding there. The next moment, he hoped she hadn't. Maybe it was better not to know, because scared or not she had to ride through. There was no other way down. Right where the poplars were growing, the cliff fell away sharply on one side, and a steep shale hill rose on the other.

Bobbi was entering the trees.

Lion felt himself sweating as he watched. He braced himself for another shot. He remembered that the poplar clump had been thick, but not all that deep — probably not more than twenty-five or thirty metres. In which case, it shouldn't be very long before Bobbi and —

Sure enough, at that moment Bobbi and Brie reappeared on the open hillside on the other side of the trees. They didn't even look flustered.

Then was he wrong about the sharpshooter still being in there?

Desperately, Lion tried to convince himself that he *was* wrong, but all he could think about was how it would feel to be shot. Like a bee sting? Worse, probably. One thing was for sure, it would knock him off Rajah. He knew that from watching TV. On TV, getting shot always knocked people off their horses.

He was almost at the poplars. He could see the opening where the path started through. He wished he could see it all the way but it twisted too much. From the ride up, he remembered that Raj should be able to go through at a gallop because the path was fairly wide. Four or five feet at least. Maybe not quite as wide as that gate in the pasture, but —

With an awful sense of déjà vu, Lion felt his heart turn to ice. What if the dumb horse decided to run a replay of the little stunt that had worked so nicely for him in the pasture this morning? When he saw that nice wide path through the poplars, what if he put on the brakes? If he did, Lion hoped the sharpshooter would be grateful. It's pretty easy to hit your target when that target obligingly falls flat on his face in the dirt at your feet.

"Give me one more break, okay?" Lion pleaded, leaning low over the horse's neck. "I know you played fair about standing still when I yelled at you, but I need one more favour. Then you can play all the games you want and I won't even complain. But please, don't stop in the middle of those poplars."

They'd reached the trees. Raj continued galloping, but his head had lifted slightly and Lion could feel the muscles of the big horse's back begin to tense. "Dumb horse!" he exploded. If only one of those super-smart safety experts had forgotten about planes and cars and invented a seat belt for saddles. Well, let the stupid animal play his tricks. He'd fool Raj. He'd stay on. Shoving his feet forward against the stirrups so he'd be ready when the brakes were applied, he tightened his legs against the saddle leathers, grabbed the horn with both hands and prayed.

Lion's legs ached from gripping the saddle so tightly, and he must have had his teeth clenched because they were starting to hurt. Another fifteen seconds and they should be safe.

Lion's teeth clamped even harder. So did his legs. He stiffened them against the stirrups.

Rajah's pace didn't slacken. If anything, it picked up. The next second, to Lion's amazement, they were through. They hadn't been shot at and he hadn't been dumped in the dirt!

He couldn't believe it. Had the sharpshooter managed to get back down the hillside without them seeing or hearing anything? Or had he been in the poplars and decided not to fire? Not that it mattered now, because the danger was over. There was no other place on the hillside where Lion could be ambushed. Everywhere else there was just cactus and sagebrush, and nobody could hide behind something like that. Lion relaxed his cramped legs, and breathed normally for the first time in minutes. He leaned forward to tell the big horse thanks.

Before the words could be spoken, Rajah's head ducked downward, his front legs went out from under him, and both horse and rider crashed painfully to the ground.

Lion heard Rajah scramble to his feet. He tried to do the same but his head hurt so much that for a moment he couldn't move. Then it was too late. As he struggled to push himself into a sitting position, something thick, heavy and foul-smelling wrapped itself around his head.

"Hey!" he yelled. "Lemme go!" But the words were muffled to a whisper. He tried to pull off whatever was over his head but something caught his arms and pinned them to his sides. The foul-smelling covering pressed closer. He couldn't seem to get any air. His chest was bursting. And then the world faded to black.

It was several moments after he swam back to consciousness before Lion dared lift his head. When he did he was sorry. Quickly he turned on his stomach. When he finally stopped throwing up, he felt better.

Thickly he tried to piece together what had happened. He

remembered getting through the poplars and thinking he was safe. He remembered leaning forward to thank Rajah for not dumping him. Then what had happened? He was positive Raj hadn't put on the brakes at a dead gallop. He knew what that felt like from this morning, and this had been different. This had felt almost as if the horse had slipped, or tripped, or —

The pieces fell into place. Maybe he wasn't an authority on B-grade Westerns, but he'd watched enough of them to guess what had happened. All he needed was the proof. Struggling to his feet, he started back along the path. He found what he was looking for about twenty feet back from where he'd been lying. At a spot where the trees were thickest, and where the path took a sudden turn so it was impossible to see around it ahead of time, a piece of rope had been tied across the path. It had been stretched from a sturdy clump of sagebrush on one side to an equally sturdy clump on the other and pulled taut at the height of a galloping horse's hoofs.

It was the last clue he needed to be convinced of the identity of the sharpshooter. Riley! The guy who was an authority on Westerns.

Slowly, things began to make sense. Riley's mom must have sent him out into the hills this morning to keep an eye on the witcher. That's why Spud had seemed so scared. Maybe she'd been planning to run away, only she knew Riley was watching her to make sure she didn't. Then he and Bobbi had ridden up. The shot hadn't been accidental. It had been deliberate — to keep them from going down and talking to the witcher, so she couldn't tell them she was scared or that she wanted to run away, or anything else.

But if Riley had been trying to get rid of them, why hadn't he let them race out of here as fast as they could gallop after he had scared them off?

Trying to think made Lion's head ache even more. In

another minute he was going to throw up again. Quickly he sat down on the hard ground and put his head between his knees.

The wave of nausea passed, and as it did another question surfaced. Why had Riley stopped only him? Why hadn't Riley tried to stop Bobbi too? And what had made Riley think they were going to ride down and talk to the witcher, anyway? They hadn't even been on their horses. He'd been setting up his camera and Bobbi had been watching him. So why would Riley suddenly decide —

Because he'd been taking a picture! For some reason Riley didn't want him to photograph Spud!

Throwing up was forgotten. That camera was worth eight hundred dollars! If Riley had damaged it, or stolen it —

Lion struggled to his feet and limped back to where Riley had jumped him. His photography bag was lying in the dirt. Quickly he rummaged through it. To his relief, the camera was still there, apparently unharmed. Lifting it out of the bag he checked it more closely. Then he understood, for the film had been removed.

For a moment Lion was amused, then he looked around for Rajah. The horse was standing patiently a couple of paces away, cropping at the few available tufts of yellowed grass. Lion paused just long enough to check the small pouch on the side of the saddle, then stooped to examine the two dark red rope burns across Rajah's forelegs. Blood was starting to trickle from them. Lion rubbed his hand gently down the off centre blaze on Raj's nose. "Dumb horse," he told him softly. "I know those rope burns hurt. I'll get something to put on them as soon as we get back."

Hitching the bulky camera bag over his shoulder and pushing it back where it wouldn't be quite so much in Rajah's way, he clambered back into the saddle. That was a mistake. He'd thought he was sore a few minutes ago, but that was before he knew what he was going to feel like now.

It took a minute to get his thoughts off all the various parts of him that were screaming, then he studied the hillside. It looked deserted. It had looked deserted the last time, he reminded himself, but he had a feeling that this time he'd be okay, because Riley had what he'd come for.

Or, at least, he thought he had.

"Why were you so long?" Bobbi asked worriedly as Lion came riding up.

Lion gave her a wry grin. "You know how it is — time flies when you're having fun."

Bobbi wasn't in the mood for jokes. For the past twenty minutes she'd been waiting at the bottom of the slope getting more and more nervous. "I was afraid something had happened to you. What have you been doing?"

"Sleeping for part of the time. Being smothered the rest."

By the time he'd explained about the rope across the trail, the smothering and the missing film, the colour had drained from Bobbi's face. "Are you sure it was Riley?"

"Not positive," Lion admitted, "because I didn't actually see him. He came up on me from behind. But who else could it have been? Obviously he was acting on his mom's orders — because they don't want us talking to the witcher."

"But why?"

"So we won't have proof for Dad that Mrs. Goodchild was lying."

For a moment Bobbi thought about what Lion had said, then she replied flatly, "And they succeeded. We haven't any proof to show Dad after all that Spud isn't too sick to leave her room."

Instead of answering, Lion fumbled with the flap on the small pouch on his saddle, took something out, then extended his hand. Lying in the palm was a cartridge of film.

"But you said Riley found your camera and took out the film — ?"

"The one he took was a brand new one that I'd just put in.

I'd taken so many pictures on the drive from Vancouver that the one of the witcher was the last on the roll."

"You mean when I was urging you to hurry you were reloading that dumb camera!"

Lion grinned. "As they say in detective shows, no point in carrying a gun if it isn't loaded."

For the first time, Bobbi smiled. "As soon as Dad comes back to the motel, we'll show him the picture so he'll know Mrs. Goodchild is lying. Then he can figure out why." She relaxed and settled back in the saddle to enjoy the ride home.

Lion watched enviously. What he wouldn't give for even one small spot on his body that didn't hurt.

It seemed a year before they reached the pasture Dad had rented for them. They unsaddled the horses and rubbed them down, then Lion washed the cuts on Rajah's legs and coated them with a thick layer of salve. It must have made the big horse feel better for he stood motionless. "First thing in the morning," Lion promised quietly, "I'll be back to put on some more."

Leaving each of the horses with a large measure of oats as a treat, Bobbi and Lion set off to walk the three blocks back to the motel. The whole time they'd been riding in from the hills, Lion had been dreaming of the moment when he could get down off Raj and away from the rubbing saddle leathers, but now that he was walking he discovered it was no improvement. He tried not to limp. "If anybody asks," he told his sister, "I'll have to be honest and say that I can't recommend this as a restful holiday."

They'd reached the final block and their motel was in sight when Lion stopped abruptly. He stared at his sister in dismay.

"Now what?" Bobbi said.

"We can't show Dad that picture to prove Mrs. Goodchild is lying because I can't develop the film. I didn't bring any developing stuff with me."

Bobbi continued walking. "Big deal. Take it to a drug store."

The concerned expression on Lion's face changed to disgust. "I was right. Some of the nuts are getting out of the O Henry bars. How many drug stores have you seen in this ghost town?"

"Other people around here must take pictures. Ask the caretaker. She'll know where you can get a film developed."

Actually it was a good idea. There had to be a place where people got their films developed. And even if he couldn't get his film developed right away, neither could Riley. Which meant it could be days before Riley found out he had an unexposed roll. After all, he wouldn't be expecting that the roll in the camera had been changed. He'd assume it was the one Lion had been using, so there would be no reason for him to look at it carefully. Of course, he could have developing equipment of his own, but Lion didn't think that was likely. Only serious photographers had their own stuff, and Riley didn't strike him as a serious photographer.

As Lion and Bobbi were coming along the sidewalk toward their motel Lion noticed that the curtain on the window of the end motel unit had been pulled back a few inches and someone was staring out. It was the mustached prospector they'd seen in the parking lot the afternoon they arrived. As he saw them looking back at him he smiled and waved, then continued to watch them as they came along the sidewalk.

For some reason it made Lion uncomfortable. "I wonder why he's so interested in us?"

"Because we're strangers. Wouldn't you be interested in strangers if you lived in a place as small as this?"

"Maybe. Does he look familiar to you?"

"No."

"He does to me."

"Because you saw him yesterday in the parking lot, dummy."

"I suppose." But Lion couldn't shake the feeling that he'd seen the man somewhere else as well.

It was well past noon when Spud and Dusty finally crept from their hiding place. Spud's face was flushed and she was excited. If only Mom and Dad were here and she could tell them.

She wanted to run and shout and tell the news to everyone, but instead she held her witching rod tightly against her body with one hand, and the dog's collar with the other and stood motionless. Was that man still out there? Was Riley? In spite of the warm noon sunlight, she shivered.

It was movement that would draw attention, she knew. So taking care to move only her head, she looked carefully around, for she mustn't be seen. Not yet. Not while she was still so close to the entrance.

At last, confident that both the watcher and Riley must have given up during the long time she and Dusty were hidden, she turned her attention away from the hills and onto the ground immediately around her. Had she left any telltale footprints or broken sage branches that would give away where they had been? She couldn't see any. Then tonight after it was dark, or first thing tomorrow morning before anyone was up she'd sneak back and finish what Dad had started.

One more glance to make sure the hillside was deserted, then letting go of Dusty's collar but still carefully guarding her rod, she set off at a run for the ranch house.

Lion and Bobbi had come all the way up the walk and the man in unit fifteen was still watching them.

"Let's ask the caretaker right now where we can get a film developed," Lion suggested, moving past their doorway and continuing on to the office next door. The next moment he pushed the office door open.

The room was empty.

"We'll have to come back," said Bobbi, turning back.

But Lion had spotted a comfortable looking sofa opposite the registration desk and was gingerly lowering himself onto the cushions. "You go back to our place if you want. This is softer than anything we've got, and I'm gonna wait right here." He reached for a stack of papers and magazines on an end table next to the sofa and started rifling through. "Maybe the caretaker lady has some comics or something."

For a moment Bobbi looked undecided. But there wasn't any real reason to go back to an empty motel room, so she joined her brother in hunting for something decent to read.

It seemed they were out of luck. Lots of outdated local newspapers, and a few People magazines, but nothing they were interested in. Lion had almost reached the bottom of the pile and was just about to give up when his eye caught a picture in one of the Quesnel newspapers. "That's him!" he exclaimed, grabbing his sister's arm with one hand and pointing with the other to a picture of the man they'd seen just a few minutes before peering out from the end apartment.

"I dunno," Bobbi said hesitantly, studying the picture.

"He's looking serious here and wearing a suit, and we've only seen him in jeans and hiking boots. But it's the same guy. I'm positive it is."

Lion's attention moved to the article accompanying the picture. "'Geological researcher and prospector O. M. Klein is presently in the Barkerville area completing a two year survey of historic gold mine sites.' I told you he was a prospector."

He continued reading. "'When contacted at the motel where he is staying Mr. Klein admitted that he has a great fondness for the region, and has tried unsuccessfully to buy ranch property here on several occasions. Just over a year ago he submitted the high bid for the ten-thousand acre Diamond A ranch, but at the last moment owner Mrs. B.V. Goodchild decided not to sell and the deal fell through. However, Mr. Klein admits he is still looking.'"

Lion read the article through a second time. Bobbi, meantime, was reading over his shoulder.

"It doesn't make sense," Lion said at last.

"Why not? What's strange about a geological engineer doing a survey of historic gold mines?"

"Not that. The business about the ranch property." Lion continued to frown. "Dad told us people around here could hardly make a living and were trying to sell their property, only nobody wanted to buy. You saw yourself how dry and rocky everything is. If this guy is dying to move here, how come everybody within fifty miles isn't rushing up to make him an offer?"

"Probably they are, but maybe he isn't willing to pay what they're asking. He doesn't look as if he's got much money."

Lion had to agree that was true. The man looked like an interesting sort of adventurer, but he didn't look very well off. Except for the Camaro.

Bobbi was watching the clock behind the registration desk. "Let's go and come back later, okay?"

Since there was nothing left to read, Lion didn't argue. Dropping the paper back on the pile, he got to his feet. Then he wished he hadn't, for he'd forgotten how much it hurt to move.

While he was still trying to recover the door opened.

Filling the doorway was the pudgy figure of the caretaker lady. At the sight of Bobbi and Lion her smile changed to a glare.

It wasn't hard to guess that she was about to bawl them out for having come into the office without permission, so before she had a chance, Lion blurted, "We knocked, but you weren't here. And we had to speak to you about something important, so we came in to wait. We've got to find out where we can get a rush —" He choked off the rest in mid-sentence, because a second figure had moved into sight behind the bulky caretaker — a familiar figure wearing an old-fashioned dirndl skirt and a shapeless grey cardigan, with her hair tied at the back of her head in a bun.

It seemed Mrs. Goodchild was as startled at seeing them as they were at seeing her. Mumbling something that included the words "must get back" she turned and hurried off.

"Needed to find out where you can get what?" the caretaker lady prompted icily.

For a moment Lion was too stunned by his near miss to think of anything to say at all. He'd been starting to ask where they could get a rush job done on film developing, rather than having to wait until they got back home to Vancouver. Was he ever glad he'd stopped in time, for that might have been enough to make Mrs. Goodchild suspicious.

He was pretty sure as soon as she got back out to the ranch Riley would be waiting to tell her about stealing the film. Since it was still in the camera, they'd both assume that the roll of film was the one Lion had been using and that it had the picture of the witcher on it. But they wouldn't assume that if Mrs. Goodchild told Riley that when she'd been in Wells a while earlier she'd overheard Lion and Bobbi making a big thing about getting a film developed in a hurry. Riley and his mom would start wondering right away if they had the right one. They'd look closely at the one they had, and Lion was willing to bet that even people who didn't know much about photography could tell whether or not a film had been started.

The face scowling down at him was growing impatient. He had to say something. "We — that is —" he stammered, "we were wondering where we could get a rush tour of the area before we have to go back to Vancouver — you know, museums and stuff. But if you're busy, we can come back later."

If there were any rush tours to museums he never found out, for he didn't listen to the answer. He was too busy trying to decide whether or not she'd believed him. He waited until she finished talking, decided she didn't look as if she was suspicious, thanked her, then with Bobbi at his heels, headed for the adjoining apartment.

He waited while Bobbi unlocked the door and let them inside, then pushing it closed he leaned against the panel. "Was that ever close. Another second and I'd have blown everything."

"Now what d'we do?" Bobbi sounded uneasy.

"Have lunch."

"Be serious."

"I am. Brain cells don't work when they're hungry. That's why Dad bought us all that stuff last night. We'll get something to eat then head out and see if anybody else in town knows where we can get a film developed — anybody who isn't a friend of Mrs. Goodchild's."

But though they spent the next two hours searching the town, asking at the other hotel, at the grocery store and at the service station, nobody developed films. Everybody insisted they'd have to send it to Quesnel.

"We can still tell Dad about the witcher being out in the hills," Bobbi said as they came back once more to the motel. "Maybe we can't show him a picture to prove it, but at least we can tell him."

Lion nodded. He was looking grim. "It's almost four. D'you figure he'll be home soon? I'd just as soon not be stuck in this motel room too long by ourselves."

Bobbi looked puzzled. "Why not?"

"Because I've got a hunch we might not stay by ourselves."

"What d'you mean?"

"Maybe Riley and Mrs. Goodchild don't need a goof up from us to make them suspicious. Maybe they've already looked carefully at that film and discovered it hasn't been used. They know where we're staying — thanks to Mrs. Goodchild's visit this morning to her caretaker friend. So don't bet your life savings against the possibility that they may be back to pay us a visit."

Bobbi was looking more and more unhappy. "Why are you so sure it was Riley who stole the film? You said you didn't actually see him. It could have been somebody else?"

"Who else would have pulled a B grade Western stunt to trip my horse?"

For a long moment Bobbi was silent. Then she said slowly, "Do you really think that if they have discovered they have the wrong film, they'll come back to try to get the right one?"

Lion nodded. He glanced carefully at the door. "It wouldn't be hard to open that ancient latch. I bet a plastic credit card would spring it easily."

Again for a moment Bobbi was silent. Then watching Lion carefully she said, "So, if they do come back for the right roll do we give it to them?"

Of course they did! Lion wanted to shout. He'd already had one taste of how rough Riley could play, and he didn't want another. A person had to look out for himself.

But if they gave up the film what would happen to the

witcher? He was remembering how lonely she looked this morning out in that silent valley. He knew how awful he felt without Mom and he still had Dad and Bobbi. The witcher didn't have anyone but the black and white dog.

Bobbi was still waiting for an answer.

"Maybe Dad'll get home first," Lion blustered to hide his feelings. "If he doesn't —" He paused, then finished in a rush, "No — we won't give up the film."

"You mean that!" Bobbi exclaimed delightedly. "You agree that we won't give them the film?"

"No matter what, we won't give it to them," Lion said, making his voice brusque and business-like so his sister wouldn't guess how much her approval meant to him. "We'll hide it. Or we'll tell them we lost it. That's it. We'll say it must have come out of my pocket when I fell off Rajah, only I didn't notice till I got home."

"What if they don't believe us?"

"If they search the place and don't find it, they'll have to believe us — at least until after they've headed out into the hills to check. And before they get back again, Dad will be home for sure."

Bobbi had to admit it was a good idea. "So where do we hide it? I know. In my suitcase."

"That's probably the first place they'll look."

"Then in Dad's."

"No better."

"How about under the rug?"

"Every spy on TV hides things either under the rug or under somebody's pillow," Lion said with disgust.

"Then you suggest something."

"The fridge."

"That's dumb."

"No it isn't. I read an article about this writer guy who used to hide his manuscripts in the fridge so nobody would steal them. He said nobody every looked there."

The more Bobbi thought about it the more she decided it might work. Wrapping the film cartridge in several plastic bags, they put it into one of Dad's brown manila business envelopes, secured it with an elastic, then tucked it at the very back of the fridge behind the cartons of milk Dad had bought for them yesterday together with some eggs, cheese, breakfast cereal, butter and bananas.

"Now what?" said Bobbi.

"We wait," Lion replied.

16

The minutes dragged.

Several times the telephone rang. Both Lion and Bobbi jumped thinking it might be Dad, but it wasn't even their phone. It was the one in the motel office. It was right next door to where they were sitting and the walls were so thin the ring carried clearly. In fact, they could almost make out what the caretaker lady was saying to the person on the other end of the line.

"You think one of those calls might be from Mrs. Goodchild?" Lion said at last.

"Why would she phone?"

"To see if we've gone out yet. They're not going to come while we're here if they can avoid it. That was the whole point behind Riley jumping me in the hills. So I wouldn't see who it was who was rifling my camera bag."

The phone rang again. Bobbi plaited nervously at the hem of her shirt. "Too bad there isn't some way we could find out for sure who's phoning."

Lion gave his sister an odd look from under half-lowered lids, then got to his feet. He disappeared into the tiny back bedroom returning a minute later with something half hidden behind his back.

"Lion! Dad will freak out if he discovers you brought that thing!"

Lion grinned. "He won't care, as long as I don't do anything really nosy. Besides, I thought you just said you wanted to find out who was phoning."

Bringing the stethoscope he was holding into full view he moved to the wall separating their motel unit from the caretaker's suite. He fastened the ear pieces into his ears, then pressed the flat sound-sensitive disc against the wall. "If this doesn't work I'll get an empty glass from the kitchen and put it against the wall first. That creates a vacuum and the sound travels lots better. I use that sometimes when you're talking really quietly on the phone."

"You eavesdrop on my phone conversations!"

"Shhh," Lion directed.

Three years ago Lion's doctor uncle had given him an old stethoscope for Christmas. Within a week he'd checked the heart sounds of every dog and cat in the neighbourhood, also Brie's, a gerbil's and a gold fish's. He'd been particularly proud of managing the gold fish. Not only because gold fish aren't that easy to hold, but because if he hadn't been quick there'd have been no heart sounds left to listen to.

Then he discovered that stethoscopes could also pick up conversations through walls and closed doors and after that listening to heart sounds sank to secondary importance.

"Who's she talking to?" Bobbi whispered.

"I can only hear her side of the conversation, dummy."

"Can't you tell who it is?"

"Shhh."

"... of course, I won't say anything if you don't want me to," the caretaker's voice came clearly through the stethoscope earpieces. "... but I think you should tell someone, Bea. There could be danger." Her voice grew even more worried. "That's what I mean ... No, not just for her — there could be danger for you too. You're a long way from town. If he should decide to take things into his own hands ... Very well, I'll keep quiet, but promise me you won't open the door to anyone till you know who it is. In fact, I don't think you should even answer the phone once it's dark. You know how clever he is. He might find some way to convince you to come out to talk to him ... All right, maybe I am being silly, but promise me you will be careful?" There was a pause as the person on the other end replied, then a click as the phone was hung up.

"Who was it? Tell me!" Bobbi said impatiently.

"Someone the caretaker called Bea." He repeated the conversation he had overheard.

"It has to be Mrs. Goodchild. Her initials were B.V. in that newspaper report, remember?"

Lion nodded. "And Spud called her Aunt Beverley in that album."

"But why would she be in danger? What does it mean?"

Lion shook his head.

The phone rang again, and this time it wasn't the phone next door. Bobbi dived for it.

It was Dad. He was still waiting to talk to the Ministry people to set up a schedule of meetings for tomorrow. As a result he wouldn't be getting home until a little later than planned. "Don't wait for me to go for supper," he added. "You two go ahead and I'll join you when I can. I've told them at the restaurant down the street to serve you whatever you want and I'll pay for it when I get there."

"That's okay Dad, we'll wait for you," Bobbi said quickly, moving the receiver a bit away from her ear so Lion could hear too. "But first there's something we want to tell you —"

"I can't stop now." Dad sounded apologetic.

"It's about Spud," Lion put in excitedly.

"We'll talk as soon as I get home," Dad went on. "Meantime, go and get yourselves a good dinner. I'll be there as soon as I can — it should be long before dark." A final apology and the line went dead.

For a moment Bobbi continued to hold the receiver as if Dad might come back, then she slowly set it down.

"What's the time?" Lion asked gruffly.

Bobbi checked her watch. "Ten past six."

"That means another hour before he gets home."

"Or longer," Bobbi added.

The telephone jangled again.

"It's Dad calling back," Lion exclaimed ashamed of the relief he felt. He grabbed the phone. But his excitement faded as he listened. He shook his head. "Sorry, he's not here. I don't think he'll be here before seven or seven thirty. At least that's what he said when he phoned a few minutes ago. Can I take a message?"

There was a pause. The colour drained from Lion's cheeks as he listened. He turned an agonized face toward his sister, then without saying another word, hung up the receiver.

"Who was it?

It was hard to make his tongue form the words. "Mrs. Goodchild. I've just told her we'll be here by ourselves for the next hour."

"Exactly what did she say?" Bobbi asked.

"Nothing that you didn't hear, except for me to tell Dad that Beverley Goodchild telephoned."

"So now they know how much time they've got." Bobbi's voice was tight.

Lion nodded. He was frightened.

"We should take the film and go some place where they can't find us," Bobbi suggested.

It was tempting. But the idea of wandering around out in the open not knowing when Riley or Mrs. Goodchild might appear seemed worse than staying where they were.

"How about giving it to that man in unit fifteen for safe keeping," Bobbi went on. "I bet anything he'd keep it for us."

Lion had to agree it was a good idea.

They took the film out of the fridge, then slipped quietly past the suite next door so the caretaker lady wouldn't see them. If she was a friend of Mrs. Goodchild's they weren't taking any chances on letting her guess what they were doing.

But before they'd gone half way along the row of motel units they knew they were wasting their time for there was no Camaro parked out front of unit fifteen and no sign of anyone inside. On the off chance that the man might be there after all, they knocked on the door, but there was no answer.

"So much for that brilliant idea," Lion muttered as they returned to their own place and put the chain back on the door. He returned the film to its hiding place behind the milk cartons. "What time is it?"

Bobbi checked her watch. "Half past six."

"You want to watch TV?"

After a few minutes they turned it off. It was too easy to get caught up in the program and forget about listening for somebody pushing up a window, or jimmying the front door.

The next hour seemed like a lifetime, particularly since the floorboards kept creaking for no reason, and noises outside sounded exactly like somebody pushing up a window. At last Bobbi's watch read half-past seven.

"We'd better take the chain off the door or Dad won't be able to get in," Lion said, moving to do so.

But they soon put it back on again.

"Should we go to the restaurant like Dad said and wait for him there?" Bobbi suggested.

"What if Riley and his mom are waiting outside for us to do that, so they can come in and search the place."

"We could take the film with us."

"How long do you figure it'll take them to decide that's what we've done? This town isn't big enough to hide in."

Bobbi decided she wasn't all that hungry after all. "Maybe we should just make something here."

"So long as it's peanut butter sandwiches."

"Why not fried eggs?"

"Because last time you made fried eggs it was a toss up between sitting down and enjoying them at the table or taking them straight to the racquetball court."

Bobbi giggled. It felt good. She felt as if she hadn't done anything but shiver for about five years. "So, okay. We'll have peanut butter sandwiches."

When they finished the sandwiches Lion suggested playing cribbage, but by eight-thirty neither of them could concentrate on the cards. Part of the trouble was that the room was so hot and stuffy. However, there was no way they were opening any doors or windows.

At nine Lion relaxed. "They can't be coming after all," he announced, getting to his feet and stretching his tense muscles. "They'd have come before this if they'd been going to. After all, they were expecting Dad to get back over an hour ago."

He was right, Bobbi decided.

"I'm making another sandwich. You want one?" Lion asked, heading for the kitchen.

But he didn't reach it because at that moment a soft creaking noise sounded in the small back bedroom.

Lion froze.

The creaking noise came again. Someone was quietly pushing open the window.

"I've an idea phoning 911 mightn't work in a ghost town," Lion said with what he hoped would pass for courage, and headed for the door.

Bobbi got there first. For an endless moment she fumbled with the chain.

"Hurry up!" Lion urged.

At last the door came open.

There was still no sign of life in unit fifteen. Lion would have headed straight over there, but the windows were still dark and the door was still closed tight. He glanced around. "There," he suggested, pointing to a shadowed spot in the parking lot with a good view of the front of the motel. "At least from there we'll be able to see who it is when they leave."

But they were disappointed. Ten minutes later when a figure emerged from the doorway, all they could see for sure was that it was only one person. They couldn't even tell through the shadows whether it was a man or a woman.

They waited another minute or two to be sure the visitor didn't come back, then cautiously made their way back to their motel unit. Timidly Lion pushed open the door. Holding his breath he turned on the light.

The place was a shambles. The furniture was upended, suitcases were open and dumped on the floor, even the beds had been torn back as if someone had been looking under the bedding.

Lion took one look then headed for the kitchen.

A moment later he reappeared in the living room. "Either Riley or his mom must have read that same article about the writer guy who used the fridge for his manuscripts," he said, his face tight.

"You mean it's gone?"

Lion nodded.

18

"We've got to clean up, and fast," Lion directed, righting an armchair that had been tossed on its side and replacing the cushions. "If Dad sees this mess and we have to explain, there's no way he'll let us out of this motel for the rest of the trip."

They managed to get the furniture back in place and the beds remade before they heard Dad's car draw up outside the door, but there was no time to pick up the clothes scattered on the bedroom floors from the dumped drawers and upended suitcases.

"Quick! Grab things and shove them in anywhere, just so they're out of sight," Lion directed.

Before they were even half done, Dad was inside.

"I trust this wasn't the result of a friendly family argument," he said dryly, surveying the mess. But there was no joking look in his eyes to accompany his words, and his mouth was grim.

Bobbi's eyes met Lion's, then they both looked back at Dad.

The grim set of Dad's mouth became grimmer. "I'm waiting for an explanation."

"We didn't do this, Dad," Bobbi said quickly. "This morning we went out on the horses, like you told us to. We went up in the hills and saw this person witching. It was Spud —"

"Mrs. Goodchild said last night that she was too ill to leave the house, but she isn't!" Lion interrupted.

Dad's face tightened even more. Lion knew that in another second he was going to say it wasn't up to Lion to make judgements about clients. Quickly, Lion blurted, "We've got proof that she isn't sick because when we saw her witching in the hills we took her picture."

The angry frown still creased Dad's face. "Whether or not Mrs. Goodchild's niece is too ill to talk to me is my business, not yours. Besides," he glanced around, "it doesn't explain this."

"Yes, it does!" Lion defended. "It was because we took Spud's picture! First they rifled my camera to get the film, then when they realized they'd got the wrong one they came here looking for the right one and trashed the apartment."

For the first time, Dad's angry scowl looked a bit uncertain. Annoyance changed to bewilderment. Again he surveyed the confusion. Then, setting down his briefcase, he sank into the armchair Lion had righted just moments before. "Maybe you'd better start at the beginning."

The breath Lion had been holding escaped in a long relieved sigh. He parked on the arm of the chair opposite Dad. "Last night when we were at the ranch I saw somebody go in the barn," he began. "I was pretty sure it was the witcher, so I went to check. I saw her in this little room at the back with the door locked."

"Do you know for certain it was locked?"

"No, but —"

"Go on."

It was better not to say anything about going inside the barn without permission, or about being followed, Lion decided. "So this morning we went out sightseeing like you told us to, and we saw the witcher again, only this time out in the hills. We took her picture because we thought that would prove to you that she wasn't sick, and that Mrs. Goodchild must have some reason for keeping her away from you, but then —" He broke off abruptly. They'd be grounded for sure if Dad found out about the rifle shot and the rope and blanket. "Only then I got careless," he substituted, turning his attention to some mud on the bottom of his jeans so he wouldn't have to meet Dad's eyes. "When I wasn't looking, somebody rifled my camera bag and stole the film. But they got the new film I'd just put into the camera, not the one with Spud's picture on it. When they discovered that's what had happened they came here and searched the apartment to get the right one." He'd run out of words.

"How do you know it was your film they were looking for?"

"It's the only thing they took."

Dad's expression was impossible to read. "If you thought the film was important and you knew they'd already tried once to get it, why didn't you put it away where it would be safe?"

Lion admitted to hiding the film in the fridge.

For the first time, Dad's expression relaxed into a smile. But next moment he was serious again. He rearranged his position in the chair until he was more comfortable. Then, in a voice heavy with sarcasm, he said, "Now perhaps you'd like to tell me the whole story, instead of just a few selected bits. Perhaps we might start with the part about not paying attention and allowing somebody to rifle your camera bag."

Lion should have known he couldn't con Dad. Actually, he was relieved to be able to tell the whole truth. He started again, and this time admitted everything. When he finished, the grim tight look was back around Dad's mouth. "If I'd had any idea that you children might be in danger," he said quietly, "I'd never have brought you here."

"We're not in danger any longer," Lion pointed out. "Now that they've got the film they aren't interested in us. And we're pretty sure we know who it is."

Dad looked surprised. "Did you see them?"

"No. But we're pretty sure it's Mrs. Goodchild and Riley."

Dad's expression hardened. "I assume you have a reason for that ridiculous accusation."

"Because they didn't want us to have proof that Mrs. Goodchild lied about Spud being too sick to talk to you," Lion defended himself quickly. "They knew if we had a picture to show you we could prove —"

"That's quite enough."

"But she did lie!" Lion insisted.

"I know she did."

That stopped Lion cold. "You know?"

"I suspected it last night, but Mrs. Goodchild admitted it to me this afternoon. She is convinced Spud is in some kind of danger. Last night when we first arrived she wasn't sure she could trust me because I was a complete stranger to her. She pretended Spud was ill because she didn't want me going anywhere near Spud until she'd —" His face broke into an amused smile. Then he continued, "Until she'd had a chance to 'check me out,' as they say on TV."

Lion was so shaken off balance by Dad's statement that Mrs. Goodchild had admitted she was lying, his mind refused to work at all for a minute. Then he understood. Mrs.

Goodchild had admitted her lie because she was clever enough to know Dad would soon work it out for himself. If she didn't admit it, Dad would stop trusting her, and if he stopped trusting her he'd never support her bid to be Spud's guardian.

"Mrs. Goodchild has agreed to bring her niece into Wells tomorrow afternoon after I get back from Quesnel," Dad continued, "so I can talk to both of them before I make my recommendation to the Ministry the following day."

Lion came back to life. "But we're practically positive Riley and Mrs. Goodchild are the ones who trashed the apartment! She came here just before lunchtime to find out which unit was ours, then late this afternoon she phoned. When she knew that you were still out and that Bobbi and I were here alone, she and Riley came —"

"That's enough!" Dad's voice was cold. He turned away. Speaking more to himself than to them, he said thoughtfully, "The thing I can't understand is why anyone would care that much about a picture."

"Because it's proof that Mrs. Goodchild is lying!" Lion insisted.

Dad didn't seem to hear. "However, if they did want that film so badly, now that they have it there should be no more danger." His attention swung back to Lion and Bobbi. "But that doesn't mean you two are to do any more amateur sleuthing." His voice was firm. "I want that clearly understood. In fact, you'd better come with me to Quesnel tomorrow morning so I can keep an eye on you."

"Quesnel?"

"I have set up meetings there with the two others who are applying for guardianship rights — the foreman in charge of Spud's parents' ranch, and Otto, that family friend who claims to have a letter of authorization. Then after that I have a short meeting scheduled with the Child Ministry people. But none of the meetings will take long. We should be back here by mid-afternoon, since Quesnel is only an hour's drive away. Then the following day I'll have to go back to make my recommendation, but after that this adoption wrangle should be satisfactorily settled."

"By the day after tomorrow?" Bobbi put in, her voice worried. "So soon?"

"The sooner it's settled the better, when a child is concerned."

"I thought you said the child welfare people might want more time to think about it, that they'd delay making a ruling —"

"That was before I heard the strong arguments the social workers have put together in support of Mrs. Goodchild's application. They are recommending her strongly. Not only because she is the only direct relative, but also because they are convinced she is devoted to the child and will give her a good home."

"But she isn't devoted to her," Bobbi insisted. "You should have seen how frightened and unhappy Spud looked today when she was out in that valley. Mrs. Goodchild wants to adopt Spud so she can make her witch for her! You said yourself there might be people like that who didn't care about looking after Spud, who just wanted to adopt her so she could look after them."

"I still think there might be," Dad returned in a calm, even tone, "but Mrs. Goodchild isn't one of them."

"How do you know?"

"Because that was precisely the reason she didn't want me coming near her niece last night — until she was sure I wasn't working with any of those people." Dad watched Bobbi and Lion thoughtfully for a moment as if wondering whether or not to go on. Then, spacing his words carefully, he continued, "Unfortunately that rumour about a cache of nuggets being hidden somewhere in the valley has frightened Mrs. Goodchild badly. Spud's reputation as a witcher is well known. Mrs. Goodchild is afraid someone might try to force her to witch for them. I'm sure she has passed her worries along to Spud to put her on her guard against strangers, which may well explain your comment about the girl looking frightened."

Lion couldn't help wondering if that was more evidence of Mrs. Goodchild's cleverness. Had she deliberately warned Spud against strangers so she'd be too scared of Dad to try to talk to him and tell him that she didn't want her aunt to adopt her? He was debating saying so aloud when Bobbi put in sharply, "But it's Mrs. Goodchild that Spud is afraid of!"

"You're talking nonsense," Dad told her firmly.

"How can you be sure it's nonsense and that Spud isn't afraid of her aunt when you haven't seen Spud or had a chance to say one word to her? And the reason you haven't is because Mrs. Goodchild has taken care not to let you!"

Lion felt like cheering. Surely that remark of Bobbi's would convince Dad of the truth. To his dismay, Dad turned away. "I don't intend to discuss this any further," he said, getting to his feet.

Bobbi was so disappointed she didn't say anything more.

Then Lion remembered the phone call. "Oh, we almost forgot," he put in. "She phoned."

Dad turned in surprise. "Mrs. Goodchild?"

Lion nodded.

"Did she leave a message?"

"No. Just to tell you she'd called." He wanted to add that the real reason was to find out if Lion and Bobbi were alone so she and Riley could come and trash the apartment, but he knew he'd be wasting his breath. Dad wasn't in the listening mood.

"She's probably calling about the meeting in Quesnel day after tomorrow," Dad went on. "I promised her I'd let her know the exact time when it's scheduled to start." He picked up the phone and dialed a number.

Bobbi moved closer to Lion. "What can we do to make Dad see that Spud's terrified of Mrs. Goodchild?"

"I don't know. For a minute I thought you had him convinced. But I don't think we should argue anymore tonight. He's pretty ticked. Already we're going to get dragged to Quesnel while he meets with those two other potential guardians. If we push anymore he might decide to keep us with him all the rest of the time we're here. Then we wouldn't be able to help anybody."

Bobbi looked as if she was going to say something more, but at that moment Dad put down the receiver. "That's odd," he said. "She made a point of asking me to be sure to call and let her know how things were progressing. Said she'd be home and close to the phone all day. I wonder why she isn't there."

Lion's eyes met Bobbi's. He knew what she was thinking — that Mrs. Goodchild and Riley hadn't got back yet from their visit to trash the apartment.

"Never mind," Dad continued, talking more to himself than to them. "I'll get back to her later this evening. But that changes the situation for you two." He looked up at Bobbi and Lion. "Mrs. Goodchild may want to come with me to the meetings in Quesnel tomorrow, in which case I won't make you two come along after all. You can take the horses and do some more sightseeing, but I want your word that for both these next two days you'll stay well clear of any possible danger. Now, let's clean up this mess," he gestured around the room, "then go for something to eat."

Long before dawn the following morning, Spud was awake, listening for any sound of movement from her aunt's bedroom. She'd been hoping Aunt Bea would go to Quesnel today with that lawyer, as she'd planned. As soon as her aunt was gone, Spud could have set out on her own errand. But last night Aunt Bea had changed her mind. She'd decided not to go to Quesnel after all. Which meant that if Spud was going to fix things for Dad, she had to slip out right now while Aunt Bea and Riley were still sleeping.

Spud couldn't help shivering in the pre-dawn darkness as she pulled on her jeans and a blouse. She quickly added a sweater — if it was this cold in her room, it would be much colder out in the hills until the sun came up. But maybe it was good to be so early, Spud consoled herself. At least if she went now, that man wouldn't be out there spying on her.

Moving to the closet she took out her witching rod. At home she'd never worried about keeping it safe, but here at Aunt Bea's it was different. Here she always took care to put it safely out of sight in the closet.

Still in her stocking feet, with her rod in one hand and her runners held in the other, she crept silently across the room and down the hall. Last night she'd wondered if she was being overly cautious checking out all the squeaky boards before she went to bed, but this morning she was glad she'd taken the trouble.

At the front door she held her breath. Would the latch grate as she opened it?

To her relief it opened soundlessly. The next moment she was outside.

Dusty came running to greet her, tail wagging.

She stooped and held him in her arms. "Shhh!" she whispered. "We've got to be quiet. You can come, but you mustn't make any noise."

Putting on her runners, she led the way across the yard, into the barn and down the passageway to the small room at the back. It was the only safe way to go. If she and Dusty headed out across the open ground they'd be in full sight should Aunt Bea or Riley happen to look out the window. And if they were seen they'd be stopped.

The door of the small room was locked of course, but the key was in the lock. Unlike the front door lock, this one did grate when she turned it, but she wasn't worried. She knew the sound wouldn't carry to the house.

Opening the door, she went inside, called Dusty to follow, then closed the door again, leaving the key in the outside lock as usual. It would be at least two hours before she and Dusty were back — perhaps longer. Riley probably wouldn't come down to the barn until after he'd had his breakfast, and she should be back before then. But in case he came earlier, she didn't want to take a chance on his noticing that the key was gone.

"Hurry, Dusty," she whispered, starting across the room. Then she stopped and looked down at her hand. She shouldn't have brought the witching rod, she realized. She should have left it in her closet where it would be safe, for she wasn't going to need it this morning. The rod had already done its job yesterday. This morning it might be in the way — she'd probably need both hands free to do what she was planning. In fact, she might not even be able to carry the rod back again. That meant leaving it out there, and she couldn't do that, for before she could get back to get it again someone else might find it!

She'd better take it back to the house right now, she decided. But the next moment she realized she couldn't do that either. The risk of waking Mrs. Goodchild or Riley was too great. She'd crept by them once this morning, but taking the rod back meant doing it twice. She'd have to leave it here in the barn. It would be safe here, she told herself.

Carefully she pushed it tight against the wall where it wouldn't be noticed. Then she moved toward the back wall where the oval rug was hanging. "Hurry, Dusty," she whispered again. There was urgency in her voice — they had to be back before anyone else was up.

It was only barely light when Lion felt his sister shaking him.

"What time is it?"

"Quarter past seven, but —"

"Quarter past seven! Are you insane? Go back to sleep." He turned over to follow his own advice.

Bobbi shook him again. "If Dad's going to Quesnel for those meetings he'll have to make an early start. We've got to talk to him before he goes and make him see that Mrs. Goodchild shouldn't be allowed to adopt Spud."

"You go talk to him," Lion muttered sleepily, pulling the covers over his ears.

Again Bobbi shook him.

"Go way!"

"No," Bobbi returned. "You said yesterday you wouldn't give up the film — you were even prepared to risk getting beaten up so we'd have proof to show Dad that the witcher wasn't sick."

"Would I ever have hated myself if that had happened." The words came indistinctly from under the blankets.

"Pardon?"

Lion pushed the covers an inch away from his mouth. "I'd have been beaten up for nothing, because Dad didn't need the proof. He already knew Mrs. Goodchild was lying." He shut his eyes. "Come back when it's morning, okay?" Turning on his side he snuggled back down under the covers.

"Lion please! You can't go back to being a bystander now."

For a moment he pretended he didn't hear, then reluctantly he turned back to face his sister. "So, what d'you want me to do."

"Get concerned."

"Because Spud is scared?"

Bobbi nodded.

Rubbing the sleep out of his eyes, Lion pushed back the covers. The trouble was he already was concerned, and he wished he wasn't. Life used to be so simple when he'd minded his own business. Now he kept seeing a small figure all alone on the hillside, hugging her dog and swiping at her eyes, and looking over her shoulder as if she was terrified, and it made him hot and uncomfortable. "So, what should we do?"

Bobbi looked so delighted Lion was afraid for a minute she might be going to hug him. "As soon as we hear Dad moving around in his room we go talk to him. At first I thought we should wait till breakfast — that's always a good time for parent-child bonding — but I've changed my mind. Breakfast could be too late. Dad might be in a hurry, and then there wouldn't be time to explain anything."

"You want to go into his room now?"

"Well — soon."

With a sigh Lion swung his feet to the floor. "Let me get dressed."

Bobbi turned to leave. At the doorway she stopped and looked back. Her face was soft. "Thanks, Lion," she told him quietly.

For some reason it suddenly seemed important to set things straight. "Remember the morning we were leaving?" he said, feeling awkward and self-conscious and deliberately concentrated on straightening the covers on his bed. He could hear Bobbi behind him in the doorway, but knew if he turned and looked at her or gave her a chance to answer he'd never have the courage to finish. "In case you're still wondering," he rushed on, "I'm glad I came." A funny note had come into his voice. He coughed to clear it, then turned back intending to tell Bobbi it was kind of neat having her for a sister, but the doorway was empty. The next moment he heard the water running in the bathroom wash-basin.

For a moment he was disappointed, then he started to grin. He reached for his clothes. Maybe it was a good thing Bobbi hadn't waited to hear what he was saying after all. Think how embarrassing it would be to have actually come out and said something dumb like that.

He put back on the jeans and shirt he'd left on the side of the bed last night. He debated about the socks. They looked kind of grungy. One more day at the most, he decided. Tomorrow for sure he'd get a clean pair. He pulled the dirty ones back on and went in search of Bobbi.

She was waiting for him in the hall. Together they moved across the hall toward Dad's room. The door was partly open.

"Sorry to wake you Dad," Bobbi began as they moved toward it, "but can we talk to you for a —"

The room was empty.

"He can't have gone already!" Bobbi said in an agonized voice. "It's not even close to eight o'clock!"

Quickly Lion checked the front window. The station wagon wasn't in its usual spot outside the door. Dad must have gone some time ago.

Bobbi looked on the brink of tears. "We should have made him listen last night, even if it did mean a major blow-up. Now it's too late. He said the case was almost settled already."

"No, he didn't." Lion tried to remember exactly what Dad had said. "I think he said today is just preliminary stuff — meetings with those two other claimants. He's not making his recommendation to the Ministry till tomorrow, so we —" The phone interrupted him.

Bobbi went to answer it. "I'm sorry, he's already left," she told the caller. There was a pause. "Yes, if he phones back I'll give him the message." She put down the receiver. "Well at least that will simplify Dad's job. That was that family friend — Otto, Dad called him. Apparently he has decided not to push for custody rights after all, in spite of his letter, and is cancelling his meeting with Dad in Quesnel this morning."

"Is that what he called himself? Just Otto?"

"Mmmm-hmmm. If Dad should phone back we're to let him know that the meeting is cancelled."

Lion nodded. Then he frowned. "That means the decision about who gets to adopt Spud is between just the ranch foreman and Mrs. Goodchild, so it's more important than ever that we find some convincing proof that Spud really is scared of her aunt."

"Only how can we do that when we've just got today." It wasn't a question, it was a statement. For the first time Bobbi sounded discouraged.

Lion felt a wave of guilt. "We'd probably have found out what we needed to know yesterday if I'd let you ride straight down and talk to the witcher when you'd wanted to," he admitted bitterly. "Only I insisted on taking that picture. And now we haven't got it anyway."

Instead of agreeing and making him feel worse, Bobbi said,

"You didn't know somebody was going to steal the picture. At the time getting proof to convince Dad was the sensible thing to do."

For a minute Lion wished he'd managed to tell her he was glad to have her as a sister after all. Maybe sometime he still would, even if it did make him feel dumb.

"So since I ruined things yesterday," he went on, "why don't we ride out there this morning and talk to her?"

"Because we gave Dad our word we'd stay out of trouble," Bobbi returned bluntly.

"How can there be any trouble if Mrs. Goodchild has gone with Dad to Quesnel."

"Riley won't have gone. What happens if we run into him?"

"We can always tell him we came to ask if he knows where we can get a film developed."

"That isn't funny!" Bobbi shivered.

Lion had joked because he didn't dare not joke. He wished his sister hadn't reminded him of Riley. He could still feel that blanket tightening over his head, but he pushed the thought away. "Riley will be busy with chores, or watching westerns on TV," he said in what he hoped was a convincing tone. "In any case, we'll keep out of his way."

It was clear Bobbi was tempted, but again she shook her head. "We promised."

"That was before we knew we weren't going to have a chance to talk to Dad this morning. If he hadn't left so early and if we'd had a chance to explain, I bet anything he'd have said we could go as long as we were careful."

Bobbi didn't agree, but she didn't disagree either.

Lion pushed his advantage. "All we need to do is repeat what we did yesterday — ride cross country. When we reach that final hill we'll go straight over it and approach the ranch yard from the back. We'll be screened by the barn. If the place is deserted we'll find Spud and talk to her, but if anybody is there — Riley or Mrs. Goodchild — we'll keep our word to Dad. We won't go any farther. We'll turn around and ride right back here again."

Bobbi's frown faded slightly. "Dad wouldn't call that dangerous or getting into trouble, would he?" she said, obviously arguing with herself. "He wouldn't mind us talking to Spud if she's there all by herself. In fact," she added warming to her argument, "once he knows the facts he'd probably be the first to say we couldn't back away and let poor Spud be adopted by Mrs. Goodchild without even trying to help."

"So shall we go?"

Bobbi nodded.

"Good. Only first I'll get some breakfast."

It had occurred to Lion as he'd been talking that the horses might start to whinny as they neared the ranch house, in which case being screened by the barn was no advantage. But there was no point in mentioning that to Bobbi, he decided. There was also no point in mentioning that though they'd be screened by the barn once they reached valley level, all the way down that long final hill they would be in clear view. It was better to leave both those things unsaid, he decided.

Fifteen minutes later they were out the door and moving across the parking lot.

At the same moment, almost as if he'd been watching for them, the prospector from unit fifteen came out of his door, again dressed in jeans and hiking boots, with binoculars slung around his neck.

"Enjoying your holiday?" he asked as their path brought them toward him.

Bobbi returned his smile. "Yes, thanks."

"I hear you're keen photographers. My friends who run the service station tell me you were inquiring yesterday about getting a film developed. Unfortunately there's no place right in Wells, but I have some business to do in Quesnel this morning. If you like I can take your film to the camera shop there and get it developed for you. The owners are friends of mine and will do it right away if I ask them."

Bobbi looked thoroughly flustered. "The thing is," she began, "we — uh —"

"Thanks anyway," Lion cut in quickly before his sister could blurt out that the film had been stolen. "But we're probably heading back to town ourselves tomorrow or Friday."

"Then I guess you won't need my help after all." The prospector's smile widened. "It's nice to see young people taking such an interest in photography. Not many have the patience to use a tripod, you know." Raising his hand in a casual wave he turned and got behind the wheel of the Camaro parked outside his door.

Lion frowned as he watched him drive away. O. M. Klein, that newspaper article said his name was. Again Lion had the nagging feeling he'd seen the man before, and not just in that Quesnel paper. He'd seen him some other place as well, only he couldn't remember where.

"I know you think Mr. Klein is being nosy," Bobbi accused, moving across the parking lot in the direction of the pasture. "But you've got to admit it was nice of him to offer to get that film developed for us."

Lion fell into step beside her. "Maybe."

"What do you mean, maybe? What's bothering you?"

"Nothing, really. Only ever since we arrived he's taken this big interest in us. Why?"

"What big interest? Apart from welcoming us to Wells, he hasn't even spoken to us till today."

It was true, Lion conceded. "Just the same — "

"How many perfect strangers go out of their way to try to help somebody they don't even know get a film developed? He's just being nice."

"I guess," Lion admitted. Still, he wished he could remember where he'd seen the man before.

21

~

Lion and Bobbi caught the horses and checked to make sure the cuts on Rajah's legs weren't serious enough to cause any problem. While Lion put on another generous coating of salve as promised, Bobbi gave both Brie and Rajah their breakfast of alfalfa hay. By a few minutes before ten they had the horses groomed and saddled and were heading off as quickly as the rocks and cactus would allow along the route they'd ridden yesterday.

They reached the top of the first ridge and continued up the slope toward the second. As they passed through the clump of poplars where the rifleman had been hiding, Lion felt the goosebumps rippling across his arms and shoulders. He was glad goosebumps didn't show through a shirt. If they did his sister might think he was scared.

They reached the spot where he'd set his camera up the previous morning.

For the past few minutes Bobbi had been looking all around, searching the dry landscape for a small redheaded figure walking slowly over the baked ground, a witching rod shaped like an upside-down letter L held in one hand. "She isn't there," she said at last in a disappointed voice.

"Of course she isn't. She's probably in that room in the barn. But even if she is out witching it won't be here. She did this area yesterday."

Bobbi had to admit he had a point.

It had been cool when they'd started out but it had taken them more than an hour to get this far. As they crossed the dry valley floor and began climbing Lion could feel his shirt starting to stick to his back.

It seemed an age before they reached the top of the second ridge of hills and finally saw below them the brown and yellow buildings of the Diamond A. This time everything was in the reverse order from when they'd driven in with Dad two nights ago. Looking down from the hilltop they were staring at the back of the barn and the cluster of chicken coups, with the ranch house a comfortable distance farther on.

Lion's attention focused on the long downhill slope stretching directly ahead of them. It would have been nice if there'd been a few big clumps of those screening poplars somewhere along here, he reflected.

The same thing must have occurred to Bobbi. "I thought you said we'd be screened by the barn." Her voice was tight.

"We will be as soon as we get down this slope."

"Then let's get down." She kicked Brie into a trot.

"Bobbi! Make your horse walk!" Lion's voice was an urgent whisper. "We don't want to phone ahead and tell Riley we're coming. Hoofbeats carry like crazy out in the open."

"But we'll be forever getting down this hill at a walk. All that time we'll be in full view of anybody looking out the ranch house windows."

"We'll just have to hope nobody looks out," Lion told her, hoping his voice sounded more confident than he was feeling.

Reluctantly Bobbi did as Lion said and drew Brie back beside Rajah.

It probably took only three or four minutes to descend the hill but it seemed like an hour. As they finally reached the bottom and moved in behind the protective cover of the barn Bobbi let her breath out in a long relieved sigh. "Did you see anybody looking?"

"No, but that doesn't mean we're safe. If Riley looked out

and saw us he wouldn't be likely to rush out and ask politely what we're doing. He'll wait till we're close enough so we can't turn and run, then grab us. That way he'll be sure he's gonna get an answer to his question."

"I'd just as soon you hadn't thought of that," Bobbi told him with a crooked smile.

Lion grinned back. "I wish I hadn't either," he admitted.

The back of the barn was now just fifty metres away. "They should cut down that bush," Bobbi whispered, pointing to a big round clump of sage growing right against the back wall of the barn. "It looks weird. But I guess nobody sees it if they come by the road as they're supposed to."

"That must be what was scratching me to pieces that first night when I was trying to look in the window," Lion said, relieved to have something to think about besides people waiting to jump out at them.

"Is that the window you looked in?" Bobbi pointed to a small window high up on the barn wall.

Lion nodded.

In spite of the heat, Bobbi shivered. "Poor Spud. I wonder if she's in there right now."

"Probably."

"What a gruesome room. One bare table, one bare chair, one bare cot and a bare floor because the rug is hanging on the wall."

So much had happened in the past day and a half that Lion had forgotten about the braid rug hanging on the wall.

He tried to remember which wall it had been on. Had he seen it when he'd been clinging to the sill and looking through the window? If so it must have been hanging on the inside wall of the room — the wall that separated that room from the rest of the barn. Or had he seen it when he'd come back with Bobbi and unlocked the door.

Now he remembered. He'd seen the rug when he'd come back with Bobbi because she'd been the one who'd first noticed it. They'd been looking into the room from the door, which meant the rug was hanging on the back wall of the room, in just about the same position as that sagebrush outside —

Lion had seen far too many TV movies not to make the connection. "There must be a secret door!" he whispered excitedly. "That's why the rug is on the wall. It hides the opening on the inside and the big sagebrush hides it on the outside! That's how Spud disappeared that first night!"

"What would be the point of them locking her in if there was a secret exit door?"

"They probably figured she wouldn't know about it."

Bobbi wasn't convinced. "Why would anybody want a secret door in a barn? In a bank vault, maybe, but not into a barn."

"Then you explain why they would hang a rug on the wall."

"Maybe to cover a break in the boards and keep the cold air out."

Lion had to admit that was probably the reason, and that his theory of a secret door was pure imagination. Still, he couldn't resist staring at the large sagebrush as they rode closer. If there was a door it would be behind that sagebrush. As soon as they drew level with it he was going to check it out, even if Bobbi did laugh at him.

They'd reached the first of the chicken coups. Another twenty metres and they'd be at the barn.

Suddenly Lion's goosebumps settled back in residence. There was still no sign of movement anywhere, and no sound but the clumping of the horses' hooves on the hard ground, but somebody was watching them. He could feel it.

Nervously he glanced around. Had something moved behind that first chicken coup? Could it be Riley, waiting for them to come a bit closer, then planning to leap out at them with that blanket?

Lion ducked low in the saddle and pulled Rajah sideways as something came flying straight for his head. But the next second he was grinning sheepishly. What had leapt out at him wasn't Riley with a blanket but a thoroughly frightened rusty brown rooster. Already it was fluttering awkwardly back around the wall of the chicken coup where it had come from.

But next second a dark shadow had started inching toward them. This time it wasn't any rooster.

Lion was just about to yell to Bobbi to swing the horses around and get out of there when the shadow emerged into full view. Again he felt sheepish, for it was the black and white dog. That was probably what had frightened the rooster, Lion realized as his heart slowed to normal. But the dog wasn't prancing and wagging its tail as it had that first evening when he'd watched it follow Spud into the barn, and it wasn't squirming and wriggling happily as it had when he'd seen it yesterday with the witcher in the valley. Instead it was panting nervously, tail tucked tight under his stomach, ears flat against the sides of his head.

Dismounting, Lion moved slowly forward, one hand held out.

For a moment it looked as if the dog was going to come up. Its tail even began to edge back out from under its stomach. But at the last moment it took a quick step backward, then turned and hurried away.

Then Lion was even more puzzled, because it only went about a dozen paces. Again it stopped, turned and stood staring back at them, almost as if it was waiting for them to do something. But they didn't have time to worry about a dog. They had to find Spud and talk to her, find out why she was frightened, then take that proof to Dad.

It was just a dozen paces now to the back wall of the barn where the big sagebrush grew. Instead of remounting, Lion moved Rajah toward it on foot. Bobbi was probably right and there was nothing there, but it won't hurt to check, he told himself defensively.

"Next week's allowance says you're wrong," Bobbi told him guessing what he was thinking,

Holding Rajah's reins in one hand, Lion pulled back the branches of the sagebrush with the other.

The wall of the barn was solid and unbroken.

"So, I owe you five bucks," he conceded, keeping his voice light so his sister wouldn't guess how disappointed he was. "Come on, we'll use the front way,"

But Bobbi kept Brie at a stand. "If you want to go that way we'd better go on foot and leave the horses here. If we take them around to the front they'll be in full sight of anybody coming near the ranch. Here they're hidden."

It made sense. The barn hid the horses from being seen from the ranch house or from the drive. "Only how can we leave them when there's nothing to tie them to?"

"They don't need to be tied."

"What a dreamer."

"It's true, they don't. All we've got to do is drop their reins and they'll stand right where they are till we come back."

"This horse!" Lion gave Rajah a withering glance. "He'll be gone before we turn around."

"No, he won't. He's a cutting horse. They're trained to stand when their lines are dropped."

"Brie isn't a cutting horse."

"No, but she's trained to ground tie." As if to prove it Bobbi dropped the reins, and without even a backward glance at her horse, started moving around the side of the barn.

For a minute longer Lion hesitated, then gingerly he let go of the reins. "I just hope she's right," he muttered to no one in particular. He let the reins dangle on the ground, but kept one hand ready to grab them again if Rajah started to move. Being stranded out here without a horse was a prospect he wasn't all that keen about.

Rajah stood motionless.

Lion moved his hand back a few inches.

The horse continued to stand.

Lion moved his face close to Rajah's. "Were you listening to what she said? Cutting horses are supposed to stand without being tied, and you're supposed to be some hot shot cutting horse, so stay right here, okay? Don't even think about moving."

Rajah's ears flicked forward briefly at Lion's voice, then settled back again. Apart from the gentle swishing of his tail across his haunches there was no other sign of movement.

With an awful feeling that he was making a great mistake, Lion moved after his sister.

By the time he'd reached the front of the barn, she had already climbed the ramp and gone inside. He followed.

Even in the daylight barns aren't the brightest of places, he discovered. But at least this time he could see clearly enough to know there was nobody hiding in any of the partitions. He wasn't about to admit it, but that was a big improvement over that first night.

"If Spud's in the barn she'll be in that back room," he told Bobbi who was waiting for him part way down the passageway. But just as he went to move past her, the sound of an approaching car broke the stillness.

Bobbi's hand closed convulsively on his arm. "Somebody's coming! Mrs. Goodchild, probably." She looked around desperately. "She'll see us if we try to get back out now! We've got to hide!"

"No, we don't," Lion said with more confidence than he was feeling. "She won't come into the barn. She probably forgot something she was supposed to take to that meeting in Quesnel and came back for it. She'll go in the house, get what she wants and head off again."

For a moment they stood in silence listening to the sound of the car coming steadily nearer. Then in a tight terrified whisper Bobbi said, "What if the horses don't stay where we left them?"

"You said they would — that they were trained to"

"I know. But what if they've moved just enough so they're no longer hidden by the barn?"

"Then we take away their licenses as cutting horses," Lion quipped trying to sound unconcerned, but it was suddenly hard to get enough air to breathe normally. If the horses had moved, and if Mrs. Goodchild saw them —

The car must have reached the turn-around in the drive because the motor tone changed as it slowed. The next moment the ignition was turned off.

The sudden silence was unnerving. "We'd better see what's going on," Lion said, moving down the barn to a stall about half way along which had a small window looking out toward the ranch house. Putting his face close against the pane, he peered through the accumulation of dirt and cobwebs. Two people were getting out of the car.

"How can you see who it is through all that dirt," Bobbi objected, moving beside him and reaching up to clear a spot on the glass.

"Don't!" Lion grabbed her arm and pulled it away. "That's exactly the sort of thing a person notices — a clean spot in the middle of a filthy window. D'you want them to know we're in here watching?"

"But you can't see —"

"Yes, I can. Anyway, you already said who it was. Mrs. Goodchild and Riley."

"Have they seen us?" Bobbi sounded scared.

Lion continued to peer through the dirty window. Then for the first time he realized he must have been holding his breath because all at once it came out in a long relieved sigh. "It's okay. They haven't seen us, and they can't have seen the horses because they're heading for the house. Like I said, they probably forgot something. As soon as they get it they'll leave again. All we've got to do is sit tight." He settled himself more comfortably against the window sill and continued to watch.

Riley was ahead of his mother leading the way. Already he was at the kitchen door. Pushing it open, he moved inside. Mrs. Goodchild followed.

"See?" Lion said as a moment later Mrs. Goodchild came back out again. "She's got whatever it was she'd forgotten. Now she'll get back in the car and as soon as Riley comes out they'll head off again."

But Mrs. Goodchild didn't get back in the car. Instead, she turned and moved across the ranch yard in a direct line with the entrance to the barn.

"She's coming in here," Bobbi said in a frightened whisper, her face next to Lion's at the dirty pane. "We've got to hide!"

Lion was clutching the edge of the window sill so tightly his fingers hurt. Had the horses moved after all? Had Mrs. Goodchild seen them? Is that why she'd changed her mind about getting back in the car? Had she seen the horses and realized he and Bobbi were here somewhere —

For the first time he began to think that nice darkness of a couple of nights ago hadn't been so bad after all.

"Come on!" Bobbi's terrified whisper brought Lion back to life. He looked around to see her starting to move down the passageway toward the small room at the back of the barn.

He grabbed her arm. "Not there. There's no way out. If we go down there and Mrs. Goodchild follows us we'll be trapped." If only that secret door really had been there, but there was no time to worry about that now. He looked around. "There!" he exclaimed, pointing to where two large box stalls opened off the central passageway part way along.

All the other stalls in the barn were standing stalls designed for horses that were tethered on short halter shanks. They had mangers at the top end and side partitions to keep the horses separate from each other, but they had nothing at the back closing them off from the central passageway itself. The two large square box stalls on the other hand had solid walls on all four sides so a horse in one of them didn't need to be tied but could move around freely. "Come on," Lion urged in a tight whisper. "At least we won't be trapped this way. We'll have a chance to run if she sees us."

Opening the door to the first box stall he darted inside, waited until Bobbi had followed, then taking care not to make any noise, carefully closed the door. "Get on the floor," he directed, his voice no more than a whisper. "Press tight against this front wall. Unless she looks straight down she won't notice us. She'll think we're just part of the shadows. Only keep your head down. Faces catch attention right off."

Mutely Bobbi obeyed.

Mrs. Goodchild had reached the ramp outside the barn door. Her footsteps rang hollow on the wood. The next moment Lion could hear her walking toward their hiding place.

He could feel Bobbi shaking. He just hoped she'd remember what he'd said about keeping her face hidden. If Mrs. Goodchild walked straight by without looking, they'd be okay. But she wasn't dumb. If she had come into the barn because she suspected they were there, she'd check the box stalls as well as the back room. Those were the only places a person could hide in the daylight.

The footsteps came closer.

Lion held his breath. Would she sense they were there? People were always talking about how that sort of thing happened —

"Spud?" Mrs. Goodchild's worried voice shattered the silence.

Lion jumped so violently he was sure Mrs. Goodchild would notice, for she was practically on top of them. But she didn't even glance toward the box stall. She continued down the passageway toward the small back room.

Was he ever glad he'd talked Bobbi out of hiding in there.

"Spud? Are you in here?" Mrs. Goodchild called again. Lion heard her turn the handle on the album room door. For what seemed like hours there was silence, then he heard the door close again. She was coming back down the passageway.

That meant Spud couldn't have been in there. Then where was she? But there was no time to think about that now. Mrs. Goodchild was coming back. Lion prayed that neither he nor Bobbi would sneeze. Maybe Mrs. Goodchild hadn't looked in the box stalls last time, but this time she would. After all, she'd checked the album room. This was the only other place.

Lion braced himself and got ready. Still keeping his face hidden, he pulled his knees under him, collected his balance and tightened every muscle. As soon as the door was open far enough, he'd jump up, yell at Bobbi to follow and start running. Mrs. Goodchild would be so surprised she'd jump back. Anybody would. Before she could recover, they'd be gone.

The footsteps moved closer. Right outside their box stall they paused. A hand closed over the door latch. Lion held his breath. The door started to push open.

At the same second hurrying footsteps sounded on the ramp outside.

"Thank goodness," Mrs. Goodchild exclaimed, forgetting about searching the box stall and pulling the door closed again. She started toward the footsteps.

Lion went weak with relief. To his embarrassment he started to shiver. He rubbed at his arms and shoulders, because this was crazy. He hadn't been shivering before. Why start now when the danger was over? He rubbed harder.

"I was so afraid something had happened," Mrs. Goodchild's relieved voice continued. "I thought —"

"I can't find her anywhere, Ma."

There was a quick intake of breath, then in a voice that sounded both disappointed and worried Mrs. Goodchild said, "I thought you had her with you." She was moving toward the barn door where Riley stood waiting. "What if something has gone wrong? She was supposed to take me out this morning and show me what she'd found, only instead she's disappeared."

"We never should have left her alone. We should have taken her with us when we went into town for those groceries." Riley sounded angry. "I told you somebody's been out in the hills watching her the past couple of days."

"Couldn't you see who it was?" Mrs. Goodchild's voice sharpened. "Can't you even guess?"

Lion inched open the box stall door so they could hear the answer.

"Whoever it was is too smart. He always takes care to be standing against the sun. All I could see was a vague outline."

"But you said he seemed familiar?"

"I'm not sure." The voices were growing fainter. "So, now what do we do?" Riley went on.

"I've been trying to decide. The only thing we can do is —"

The words faded completely as they moved down the ramp and into the ranch yard.

Stiffly Bobbi got to her feet. "D'you think Spud's run away?"

Lion didn't answer. He was remembering the black and white dog. Had it looked so unhappy because Spud had run away and left it behind, or was something wrong?

"She must have run away," Bobbi decided, and for the first time all morning her voice sounded normal. "She was scared of Mrs. Goodchild, and she was afraid the Ministry people were going to give guardianship rights to her aunt tomorrow because of those arguments Dad said the social workers had put up, so she took off. Now we can stop worrying." She brushed the dirt from the knees of her riding jeans.

Lion was still puzzling. "Riley said somebody had been out in the hills watching her. Who d'you suppose it was?"

"Maybe that ranch foreman. Or maybe some complete stranger. But it doesn't matter any longer. I bet right this minute she's half way back to her family ranch in Quesnel."

"Maybe. Just so long as it isn't to that so-called family friend who's such a good friend that he phoned this morning to say he's no longer interested in adopting." Lion's voice was acid. Then a new thought struck and he started to frown. "If she's gone back to her ranch why didn't she take her dog?"

"Maybe she was planning to hitch hike, or catch a bus, and you can't take a dog on the bus."

Maybe, but Lion wasn't convinced.

"You want to check that back room just to make sure she isn't there?" he asked at his most casual.

Bobbi wasn't fooled. "You mean do I want to check that room to make double sure there isn't a secret door?" she teased. "Okay, Sherlock. Why not. At least then you'll be satisfied."

Grinning sheepishly Lion led the way down the passageway.

The room looked just as it had two evenings before — the bare cot in one corner, the chair by the oilcloth-covered table, the braid rug hanging on the wall behind the table. Even the album was still in view. The only difference was that the half-eaten apple was wizened and brown.

No, something else was different, too. On the floor in the corner just beyond where the braid rug was hanging lay a jointed metal rod shaped like a capital letter L, with a drawstring pouch attached to one arm. It looked as if it had been placed there carefully so it would be safe and out of the way. Lion picked it up. Easing open the drawstring closure he tipped some of the contents into the palm of his hand. Gold dust. Dad had told them that day when they'd been talking that witchers put some of whatever it was they were trying to find in a pouch on one end of their witching rod. Then by the electricity in their bodies they could feel a pull or a response if the other end of the rod located any of the same substance in the ground.

He put the rod back where it had been lying and moved toward the braid rug. He edged it back from where it was hanging.

There was no secret door.

But there were also no holes in the wood that let cold air through as Bobbi had suggested. Lion scowled. So why would anybody hang a rug on the wall behind a table when they needed it so much more on the —

It was as if he'd just had his ticket drawn in the lottery. He knew why the rug was hanging there! To hide a small round ring that had been sunk into the floor right where the wall joined it. Even without the rug in place the ring was hardly noticeable. A person would have to be looking for it or they'd never notice it. With the rug in place, the ring was completely hidden.

Dropping on his knees Lion slipped his fingers through the ring and lifted. A square section of flooring came away.

"Bobbi! Look! That's how Spud and the dog disappeared! They got out of the barn through this trap door!" Directly under the trap door was a square hole, perhaps four feet in each direction. It was deep enough so a person could stand upright, and led into an underground passage.

Bobbi was on her knees beside him. "Then she couldn't have been locked in," she said slowly. "Not with this trap door here."

"She could if Riley didn't know about it," Lion argued. "Maybe she'd been shut in the room a lot, and like us looked to see why the rug was hanging on the wall. Maybe she found the trap door by accident. Maybe neither Riley nor his mom knew anything about it."

"It's possible," Bobbi agreed.

"I'm going to see where it goes."

"Lion! Don't be crazy!" Bobbi reached out to grab him. "You know what Dad said about rotten timbers."

"These can't be rotten or the witcher wouldn't have used it as an escape route." Shaking off her hand, Lion dropped down into the opening. "Hey! I can see daylight!" His voice sounded hollow and slightly echo-ey. "There's a way up right here!" He moved toward it. There was a pause. Then in a voice that sounded even more hollow and farther away he added, "But the passage goes on beyond the opening. I want to see where it leads. I'm going to follow it."

"Lion don't!" Bobbi pleaded.

There was no answer.

A few minutes later, just as Bobbi was starting to panic, Lion's head reappeared in the opening. "I need a flashlight. It's an underground tunnel that goes way out into the middle of the ranch yard, but it's too dark to see anything and I'd hate to trip over something and break my neck."

"Trip over would be better than trip into," Bobbi said in a voice that wasn't quite steady. "What if in the dark that passageway you were following suddenly turned into a hole, or a pool of underground water, and you fell in before you knew it was there? What if you couldn't get out?"

Lion grinned sheepishly. "I thought of that." He clambered back out and brushed off his jeans. "At least now I can stop wondering if I just imagined I saw Spud in this back room." His face brightened. "And I don't owe you that five bucks. There's a quick way up into the yard through that sagebrush as well as the tunnel that goes farther out."

"Then why didn't you see it when you looked?"

"Because I looked in the wrong place. Instead of looking behind the sagebrush I should have looked under it. Though," he added as an after thought, "I guess that's why they picked sagebrush."

Bobbi looked even more puzzled.

"It's so stiff and prickly nobody in their right mind is going to go poking underneath it unless they have to."

"How can there be an opening underneath a big sagebrush? It'd fall into the hole."

"No, it wouldn't. Not sagebrush. That's probably another reason for picking it. The root system spreads really wide. There's lots of room in between the roots for a small opening." He grinned at his sister. "Come on. I'll show you."

"No way. I'll take your word for it."

"Aren't you planning to come with me? We've got to talk to Dad as soon as he gets back from meeting with those Social Services people. Otherwise it could be too late."

"We don't have to talk to him any longer. Spud's solved her own problems."

Lion's face sobered. "How long d'you think they'll stay solved once Mrs. Goodchild is her legal guardian and can drag her back here?"

"Oh." Bobbi's voice went flat.

"So, come on." He moved toward the trap door.

"Not that way!" Bobbi protested. "I'm not going down that hole and I'm not crawling out through any sagebrush. Besides, how would we close the door after us?"

"Easy. Just let it down over our heads."

"Then we couldn't see."

"Probably not. But it's only a couple of dozen steps."

"I'm still not going."

The grin came back into Lion's face. "I've an idea you're gonna have to. We haven't heard the sound of any car leaving, so Mrs. Goodchild and Riley are still here. If we go out by the regular way they'll see us."

Bobbi's heart plunged. What a choice. Dark and prickles or Mrs. Goodchild and Riley.

Knees shaking she climbed down into the opening under the trap door, waited while Lion checked to make sure the rug was hanging properly then followed her down and eased the square of flooring back in place over their heads.

The dark was chilling. It was also smothering and claustrophobic. Bobbi felt herself starting to panic. How could anyone have gone into a mine shaft, no matter how many fortunes were waiting there?

"Don't be scared, Bobbi." Lion's voice was reassuring in the darkness. "You want to take my hand?" His fingers closed around hers.

Gratefully Bobbi clung.

Together they inched through the blackness across the dirt floor.

"Okay, we're almost there." Lion's voice came through Bobbi's terror. "See that bit of light? That's the opening."

A moment earlier Bobbi's chest had felt as if it would explode, but, miraculously, at the sight of that small shaft of daylight she could breathe normally again. But she didn't let go of Lion's hand — not until she was directly under the opening and could see overhead the spider web of roots and above that the round grey ball of sagebrush.

"You okay now?"

"I think so."

"Then I'll go first and hold back the branches so you won't get scratched."

They crawled out from under the large sprawling lower branches of the scrubby desert plant, under the bemused eyes of Brie and Rajah, who were standing exactly where Bobbi and Lion had left them.

21

Taking care to keep the barn in between them and the ranch house, Bobbi and Lion galloped as fast as they could back toward the ridge of hills. They knew they shouldn't be galloping. They knew they shouldn't even be trotting. The only way to avoid being heard was to walk, but there was no way they could do that. Not when their backs would be to the ranch and they wouldn't know if they were being watched or followed.

But as soon as they reached the first ridge of hillocks where they were safely out of sight, Lion called Bobbi to stop.

"Why?"

"Because we've got to think."

"I thought you said we had to get back to town in a hurry and tell Dad that Spud has run away, so he can do something before the adoption ruling is decided tomorrow."

"I know I did." Moving Rajah to a spot where there were a few blades of withered yellow grass, Lion loosened the reins so he could graze. "But what if she hasn't."

"Hasn't run away?"

Lion nodded.

"But we just heard Mrs. Goodchild tell Riley that she has."

"No, we didn't. We heard her tell him she'd disappeared. That's not the same thing."

Though Bobbi had brought Brie to a stand, it had been clear from the way she continued to hold the mare up on her bit that she was impatient to get moving again. Now she moved Brie beside Rajah and relaxed her rein. "So what are you saying?"

Lion shook his head. Swinging down out of the saddle he pulled a blade of grass from its shaft, put the soft end between his teeth and sat down on the hard ground. "That's the trouble. I don't know. But something's wrong."

Bobbi stared at him for a minute with a puzzled frown, then dismounted, dropped Brie's reins so she could graze, and sat down on the ground beside him. "Something's wrong like what?"

Lion gave her a grateful smile, then went back to scowling. He dug one heel into the dirt. "For one thing, the dog. No matter what you say about not being able to take a dog on the bus, it doesn't make sense that Spud would take off and leave her dog with people she's scared of. Would you? How would you know they'd even feed it? If they were mad at you for running off they might decide to take it out on your dog."

Bobbi didn't answer. But she didn't argue either.

"Then there's the witching rod." Lion made the hole under his heel deeper. "You can take a metal rod on a bus. If she's as good at finding things with it as Dad says, why would she take off and leave it behind?"

"You don't think she's run away?"

Lion shook his head.

"Then where is she?"

That of course was the question.

Lion unsheathed another blade of grass and started chewing. "Maybe she's hiding," he said slowly.

"Why?"

That's what he didn't know. "Let's go back over everything and see if we can work it out."

But Bobbi had had enough. "There's no way you and I are going to work out anything," she said getting to her feet. "All we can do is ride back to town and tell Dad about Spud running away, then leave it to him to find out what's going on." She swung into the saddle.

"Great. And just how do you plan to make him believe us?"

It was obvious Bobbi hadn't thought of that.

"It's why we came out here this morning, remember? We were gonna talk to Spud and find out why she was scared, so we'd have some proof for Dad. D'you think he'd believe a wild story from us about Spud running away when all Mrs. Goodchild has to say is that Spud and Riley are off on a picnic somewhere, or visiting a friend?"

Again Bobbi dismounted. This time she loosened Brie's girth so the mare could relax for a bit, then sat back down on the ground. "So what do we do?"

"Get some proof and then ride into town."

"What kind of proof?"

"I dunno."

"Well, you better hurry up and decide."

Lion's attention returned to the heel that was burrowing into the dirt. "Maybe if we go over everything we know, something will jump out at us," he said slowly. "For starters we know Spud has disappeared, only she hasn't taken her dog or her witching rod so we aren't sure she's run away."

"We also know Mrs. Goodchild and Riley are worried about it," Bobbi put in.

"And that Spud found something," Lion went on, his voice starting to rise with excitement. "I forgot about that till right now, but Mrs. Goodchild said Spud was supposed to show her what she'd found this morning, only instead she took off."

"Then that proves she's run away," Bobbi argued. "She found something, didn't want to give it to Mrs. Goodchild and ran away."

Lion shook his head. "What about the dog and the witching rod."

For a moment that seemed to put the cap on the idea bottle. They both sat glowering at the ground. Then Lion said,

"Maybe we should go at this another way. Like journalists."

"What have journalists got to do with it?"

"When we were putting out the school paper last term our teacher said journalists never wrote anything till they had all the facts. And the way they got all the facts was with the five W's."

"Who, What, When, Where and Why?"

Lion grinned. He didn't think his sister would know what the five W's were. "Let's try it, okay? First, Who. That's Spud of course."

"And What is that she's disappeared."

Lion nodded. "When?"

"This isn't getting us anywhere," Bobbi protested. "When is this morning, which doesn't help us at all. As for Where and Why, we haven't got a clue about either of them."

"So, we change the second question and go at it again. At least that's what our teacher said to do."

"You mean change What?"

"Mmm-hmmm. Since 'disappeared' leads us nowhere, let's change What to 'found something.'"

"We can't answer When for that either."

"Yes, we can." Lion's mind was racing. Maybe the five W's were an okay system after all. "When has to be sometime yesterday because she told Mrs. Goodchild about it last night."

"Then maybe Where is out tromping around the deserted valley where we saw her," Bobbi put in excitedly.

"Bingo! And Why could be because she had her witching rod with her."

Now even Bobbi was starting to get excited. "You mean she could have found those nuggets Dad was talking about? Or a missed vein of gold or something?"

"Why not? Maybe she managed to keep quiet about it till after supper, except finally Mrs. Goodchild made her talk. Only by then it was too late and too dark to go back out in the hills, so Mrs. Goodchild put it off till this morning."

"But Spud fooled her by getting up early and running away," Bobbi said delightedly.

The excitement faded from Lion's face. He stopped pacing and sat back down. "That's what doesn't make sense. She should have got up and run away, only we've already decided she couldn't have because of the dog and the witching rod."

"So we're back at square one." Bobbi's voice was discouraged.

"Then we've got to change another question. Maybe we should go back to our first What."

"You mean 'disappeared' instead of 'found something'? I thought we decided 'disappeared' wasn't going to lead anywhere."

"Maybe we didn't take it far enough. That's another thing our teacher said — that sometimes things get in the way and your thoughts can't go any farther. When that happens you've got to think wide." Getting to his feet Lion again began pacing. "How do people disappear?"

"They cover themselves with invisible paint or get aliens to abduct them," Bobbi replied.

"Or they crawl through trap doors under barn floors," Lion added, matching her grin. "Come to think of it, people out here are pretty good at disappearing. This is the third time for Spud. First that night in the barn, then yesterday in the hills when we heard that shot, and now —"

Lion stopped pacing and turned a frowning face toward his sister. "Maybe that's where she's disappeared to." His voice was slow and thoughtful. "Into the same place she disappeared yesterday when that shot was fired."

Moving over to Rajah he tossed the reins over the horse's neck and prepared to mount. "Come on. Let's go see. It's only in the next valley."

But before he could swing up into the saddle, Bobbi caught his arm. "Somebody's coming!" she said in a low urgent voice.

Lion could hear something now too. A car motor. Faint, but clearly a car motor coming along the road from the direction of the ranch.

"Boy, are we ever lucky we stopped behind these hillocks," he said, "instead of back there in the open. We'd have been seen for sure if we'd been back there."

"D'you think it's Mrs. Goodchild?"

"And Riley, probably. Looking for Spud." He was remembering the blanket treatment. "We can't let them see us. But if we don't want to bump into them by accident, we've got to know where they're headed." Rearranging his reins, he swung up into the saddle. "Wait here. I'll sneak up to the top of the hill and find out."

Carefully he moved Rajah up the slope. But even before he reached the top of the rise he swung Rajah wildly sideways, then crouching low in the saddle galloped furiously back to where Bobbi and Brie were waiting.

"It's them! They were staring right at me! And they're not looking for Spud, they're after us!" His face was white. "We've got to get out of here."

Grabbing her reins Bobbi tossed them over Brie's head. Why had she loosened the girth? Her fingers were shaking so badly it was impossible to pull it tight again. "How do you know they're looking for us?"

"Because they weren't on the road. They were driving cross-country." Lion's voice was tight. "When they saw me they swung the car around and headed straight for me, yelling and waving."

"But how would they know we were here?" Bobbi said. At last she'd got the girth leathers into their proper notches. She reached for the stirrup.

"They must have heard us galloping away from the barn and followed. But stop talking and hurry up!" As he spoke, Lion moved Rajah away.

Bobbi hurried to catch up. "Hurry up where?"

"Anywhere that's rocky and sage-brushy where a car can't follow. We've got to lose them. Then we can circle back to that valley and see if we're right about where Spud disappeared to."

23

It took fifteen minutes of dodging between rocks and sagebrush and climbing shale covered hills, but at last Lion was sure the car wasn't following any longer. "Now we can go and check out that valley."

"Great," Bobbi told him. "If we can find it. After all that zigzagging I don't even know where we are."

Lion looked around. For the first time he realized he didn't know where they were either. But one thing he did know. Horses were supposed to be able to find their way back to the stable where the food was. Every book about horses said so. Right now these horses knew their food was in that pasture in Wells, and that was somewhere on the other side of that valley where Spud had been witching.

He told Bobbi what he was thinking. "So, all we've gotta do is tell these horses to take us home. In order to get there, they'll have to take us through that valley." As he spoke he let the reins go slack over Rajah's neck. "So, go home, okay?" Lion directed.

Rajah continued in the direction they were going.

Bobbi chuckled. "You sound like you're talking to a dog."

"Then you tell him."

"I can't. Not when you're riding him. He assumes you're in command."

"He knows I haven't been in command since the moment I got him," Lion said bitterly.

Again Bobbi struggled not to laugh. "He obeys you fine as long as you tell him to do things he's already decided he wants to do. Right now I bet anything he wants to go home."

"Then why didn't he go when I told him to?"

"You didn't tell him in a way he can understand. You've got to let him know that you really want him to take over."

"How?"

"First, pull him up."

Lion brought Rajah to a stand.

"Now drop your reins."

With some misgivings, Lion let the reins fall onto Rajah's neck. He had an awful suspicion that in about one more second the horse would head off at a gallop. Instead, Rajah swung his head around and looked at him.

"Leave your reins down and give him a kick," Bobbi directed.

"Are you crazy? After what happened in the pasture?"

"A gentle kick, dummy. Not as if you're trying to win the Grand National. Just sort of nudge him forward and let him go where he wants. I'll do the same with Brie."

Expecting at any moment to be at full gallop, Lion did what he was told. For a minute Rajah didn't move at all, then he took a few lazy steps. So did Brie. It looked as if they were both interested only in finding clumps of wizened yellow grass to eat. But gradually their movements seemed to be taking them in a definite direction. Ten minutes later they came around a small hillock and Lion recognized where they were.

"Hey! It worked!" He tightened his rein. "Over there is the valley where Spud was witching. Remember? We were up there when we took her picture." He pointed to a hill on their left. "By that flat spot." Moving Rajah forward he continued along the valley floor until they were in line with the spot he was using for a marker. "Spud would have been just about here," he said.

He pulled Rajah to a stop and looked around. Nothing but dry ground and clumps of sagebrush.

"Scrap one famous theory about where people disappear to," Bobbi said dryly. "Wherever Spud's gone, it isn't out here. She must have just taken off yesterday, only we didn't notice."

Lion felt like a balloon whose string had just come untied. Nobody could be hiding in this valley. The closest hill was five hundred metres away, the biggest rock in sight was no bigger than a basketball, and though the sagebrush was big, it was so dry and prickly you could see right through it. Nobody could be hiding behind —

Not behind! Underneath! Like that sagebrush by the barn!

"Bobbi! Wait!" Lion called as Bobbi started to move Brie away. He was so excited the words tumbled out. "Remember that trap door we came through in the barn? If they used a sagebrush there to hide the outside exit, why couldn't they have used one here to hide the entrance to an old mine shaft?"

"How could there be an abandoned mine shaft out in this deserted area?"

"Dad said there were deserted shafts all over. What if Spud knew about the old mine shaft but hadn't ever gone down it for the same reason Dad said we weren't to. Only yesterday when that shot was fired she ducked down without thinking." Lion's thoughts were racing faster and faster. "Remember what Dad said about how witchers found things? He said they felt a reaction when one end of their rod got close to some of the same thing they had in that pouch on the other end. We know Spud had gold dust in her pouch because we saw it this morning. What if when she ducked down

that abandoned shaft carrying her witching rod she acciden-
tally passed close to where those nuggets were hidden and
her rod started reacting?"

Bobbi's eyes were huge. "She'd know right away that she
must have stumbled on the nuggets!"

"We've got to find that shaft before Mrs. Goodchild and
Riley come back looking for us." He swung to the ground.
"There wouldn't have been time for Spud to have run very
far after that shot was fired or we'd have seen her."

Dropping Rajah's reins he looked around. "If my hunch is
right and she did duck under a sagebrush into a deserted
mine shaft, that sagebrush had to be within about a dozen
paces of where she was standing, or she wouldn't have had
time to get out of sight. Let's start from here," he pointed to
a spot a short distance away, "then move in a circle checking
every bush till we find the right one." As he spoke he reached
for the closest clump of sagebrush, pushed away the bottom
branches and peered under.

Bobbi moved to help.

"Ignore the little ones," Lion directed, checking under
another large bush. "Concentrate on ones like that one against
the barn."

They checked bush after bush with no results.

"Yuck," Bobbi exclaimed in disgust, stopping to pull a
prickle out of her finger. "The trouble is it's the big ones that
are so prickly." With the toe of her boot she nudged at a
large piece of broken glass half buried in the ground by the
sagebrush roots. "That's about a dozen broken beer bottles
I've almost tripped over in the last five minutes. Why do
people always have to litter?"

"Somebody was probably using them for target practice,"
Lion suggested. "That's probably why they're broken." He
bent and picked up the lower branches of another bush. "But
worry about the environment later. Right now we've got to
find — Bobbi! — I think this is it!"

Set into the ground underneath the bush's prickly lower branches was a square piece of wood exactly like the cover over the trap door in Mrs.Goodchild's barn. It even had an identical ring set in it.

Only this trap door couldn't be lifted. It was locked down by a heavy metal bar which went right across the top, through the ring in the centre, then was padlocked on either side to metal spikes that had been driven into the ground.

Lion stared at the locked opening. The wooden cover was grey and weathered and the ring was yellow with rust. It must have been sealed up for decades. If the witcher had ducked into a deserted mine shaft yesterday when that shot was fired it couldn't have been this one.

He was so disappointed he felt sick. But there were lots more sagebrushes to check. They'd just have to look harder.

He was moving away when his attention was caught by the padlocks. How come the wood cover was weathered and the ring was rusted but the padlocks were shiny? If everything else had rusted, how come they hadn't?

Stretching flat on the ground Lion put his face close to the wooden cover. "Spud?" he called. "Are you there?"

Silence.

Bobbi looked as disappointed as he was. "I thought for a minute we'd found her too. We'll just have to keep looking." She moved on to another sagebrush.

But Lion was still stretched on the ground. He rapped with his knuckles on the wood cover.

Again the answer was silence.

"I think we're wasting time, Lion." Bobbi's voice was anxious. "Let's ride back to town right now and find Dad."

But Lion had pressed even closer to the ground, this time with his ear to the worn wood cover. "I think I heard something!" Again he rapped.

A soft answering rap came back to them.

"She's in there!" Lion cried. "Spud, is that you?" Again he rapped on the wood.

This time it sounded as if something had been thrown gently up against the mine shaft cover — a pebble perhaps.

Sitting up, Lion began pulling frantically at the metal bar. "No wonder the dog was so upset," he said grimly.

Bobbi ran over to help. But after a moment Lion stopped pulling. He looked at his sister with a white, worried face, for he'd remembered what Dad had said. "Maybe we should go at it more carefully. Maybe that's the reason Spud's afraid to knock hard on the wood or shout back. If the timbers are rotten even the little bit of thumping we're doing might be making clusters of dirt and pebbles fall down inside. One really big thump from up here could bring the whole place down on her."

Bobbi froze. Gingerly she got to her feet. She had a sudden memory of those claustrophobic minutes when she'd been underground as they were coming out of the barn. Her throat closed convulsively. How long had Spud been in there? "We've got to get help," she said in a tight voice. "One of us has to stay here and talk to her so she knows she's not all alone, but the other's got to ride to town to get Dad. What time is it?"

Lion looked at his watch. "Half past twelve."

"Dad should be back in another half hour. Or he will be by the time one of us gets there. He said those meetings were to be over by noon, and Quesnel is only an hour's drive away."

"You ride," Lion said. "You'll make it faster." He got carefully to his feet, then moved to catch Rajah's reins. "Only let me grab this guy first."

"He won't go anywhere. He proved that when we left him behind the barn."

"Don't count on it. He likes you better than me. He might decide to go with you."

Bobbi gave him a disgusted look, then swung up into the saddle. "I'll be as fast as I can. Tell Spud to hang on." Swinging

Brie around she walked her slowly and carefully until they were well clear of where she figured the mine shaft would be, then put the mare into a canter. A moment later she was heading up the ridge.

Lion waited until she was out of sight, then gingerly relaxed his hold on Rajah's reins. Eyeing the big horse carefully, he dropped the reins on the ground. "So, you gonna stay, or what?" he said.

Rajah gazed back at him innocently.

Lion moved a step away, but he kept his hand ready. Rajah looked too innocent.

The big horse continued to stand.

If he'd been going to take off, he'd have taken off by now, Lion told himself. With a final scowl that he hoped conveyed all sorts of dire threats, he turned and sat back down by the buried mine entrance. "My sister's gone for help," he called, gently this time, his lips close to the wooden cover. "She won't be long. In just a little while we'll get you out."

Only what if the meetings with the ranch foreman and with those Ministry people in Quesnel had taken longer than Dad thought? After all, things had gone on longer than he thought they would at supper time last night.

He pushed the thought away. Even if the meetings went on until one o'clock, Dad would still be back at the motel by two, and it would take Bobbi almost that long to get there on Brie. Again he glanced at his watch. It was ten to one.

The next ninety minutes were the longest he could ever remember. Every little while he called again to Spud so she'd know he was still there, but the answering taps seemed increasingly faint and far away. Gradually the truth forced itself into his thoughts that maybe Dad hadn't come back yet — maybe he was still in Quesnel.

Just when he was sure he couldn't wait another second, his ears caught the sound he'd been waiting for. A car motor. "They're here, Spud!" he called excitedly. "My sister and my

dad. Just a couple more minutes and we'll have you out!"
Jumping to his feet he ran out from behind the sagebrush to
where he'd have a clear view of the road.

But the car speeding across the sun baked valley floor wasn't
Dad's station wagon. It was a red Camaro.

24

Lion tried to push away his disappointment. He wasn't about
to admit it, but he'd been counting on Dad taking over. Well,
it was all right. Dad would be here in a few minutes. In the
meantime, he'd get Mr. Klein to help. Actually it didn't matter who it was just so long as they could help him get that
mine cover open.

For a second the thought surfaced that this was a funny
place for Mr. Klein to be. He too had said he was going to be
in Quesnel this morning. Besides, why drive a shiny new
Camaro cross-country over rocks and sagebrush when there's
a road just a mile or so away? But Lion could worry about
those questions later. Right now he had to make sure Mr.
Klein saw him and stopped.

Frantically he started to wave. What if Mr. Klein didn't
see him? What if he continued past —

It was all right. The Camaro was headed straight for him.
With a screech of tires on pebbles, the car swerved, cornered,
then skidded to a stop beside him.

"Don't tell me you're out here taking pictures again," Mr. Klein said in an oddly irritated voice through the rolled down window. He glanced around. "Where's your camera?"

Vaguely Lion wondered why Mr. Klein should be mad. He'd said this morning that he thought picture taking was great. But there was no time to worry about that, either. "I didn't come out here to take pictures," he said quickly. "There's a girl trapped in an abandoned mine shaft. If you'd help me —"

"You watch too much TV. No one is trapped in any mine shaft —"

"Yes, she is! Over there!" Lion pointed. "The opening's under that sagebrush!" Why wouldn't Mr. Klein believe him? Why was he wasting time?

"I see." The prospector's voice held a funny ring. He was staring at the sagebrush. "And you think if the two of us work together we could get her out?"

"Yes, only hurry!" Any minute now Mrs. Goodchild and Riley could be back. This was Mrs. Goodchild's property. She could make them leave. If she did, and if the air in that shaft was just about used up — Just thinking about it made it hard to breathe properly.

"Let's see what we can do." Turning off the ignition, Mr. Klein got out of the car.

Lion was so relieved he practically cheered. "Over here," he directed, leading the way toward the large sagebrush. Dropping on his knees he pulled back the lower branches revealing the sealed wooden cover. "I get answering knocks when I bang on that wood, but they're getting fainter."

He continued to hold back the branches of the sagebrush waiting for Mr. Klein to kneel down beside him. But the geologist didn't. He didn't even glance at the wooden trap door. Instead he was staring straight at Lion, and though he was still smiling, the smile no longer reached his eyes. They had turned cold and measuring.

All at once Lion felt uncomfortable. But that was crazy, he told himself. Mr. Klein had gone out of his way to be friendly. Take this morning, the way he'd offered to get their film developed, and praised them for using a tripod —

How could he have known!

The thought jumped out of nowhere.

Lion went icy cold. The only way Mr. Klein could have known they'd used a tripod was if he'd been out in the hills watching. Just as the only way he'd have asked a minute ago if Lion was taking pictures "out here again" was if he'd seen them in this valley yesterday.

"It was you who fired at us!" he exclaimed before he could stop himself.

The smile on Klein's face broadened.

Now Lion remembered where he'd seen the geologist before. He was in those pictures in Spud's album! "You're the family friend Dad talked about — the one who has been opposing Mrs. Goodchild's adoption bid. Spud called you Otto in the album. That's what the O in your name stands for!"

Instead of being upset by Lion's words, the geologist seemed amused. "How unfortunate you didn't work out all of that yesterday, or even half an hour ago. What a shame you waited until it was too late."

Lion hardly heard Klein's words. His mind was too busy. "That's why you phoned this morning, isn't it? You'd just come back from sealing Spud down this shaft and you knew if you didn't cancel your adoption bid and your meeting with Dad, it would draw attention to you."

A look of reluctant admiration crossed Klein's face. "What a shame we haven't met under different circumstances; it's too bad to have to get rid of a smart boy like you. Yes, that's exactly why I phoned. And it is also why I told you and your sister that I was going to Quesnel this morning and could take your film to be developed." Klein's admiration changed to smug self-satisfaction. "Of course we all knew you no longer had your film, but it established a nice alibi. It placed me safely off in Quesnel all morning, and nowhere near Diamond A property, where a foolish witcher was getting herself trapped down a deserted mine shaft."

Lion's mind was racing. Klein had been in the hills yesterday — that's why Spud had been so nervous. Klein had seen Bobbi and Lion taking Spud's picture, so he'd fired that shot to scare them away. Then he'd tripped Rajah, smothered Lion and stolen the roll of film. When he'd discovered it wasn't the right roll, he had rifled their apartment. But why all that fuss about a snapshot?

"Why did you care if I took Spud's picture?" The words were out before Lion could stop them. "Why did it matter so much that you shot at us?"

For a moment, genuine surprise registered on Klein's face, as if he couldn't believe anyone would need to ask why. "Because — " he began, then broke off.

Suddenly, Lion knew why. Out of nowhere came the conviction that it wasn't the picture of Spud that Klein was worried about. It was the picture of the place where Spud was witching. *Klein was afraid that if someone saw the picture, they'd guess that the hidden mine entrance was close by!*

Everything fell into place. "That newspaper said you were doing a survey of deserted mines," Lion rushed on, "but that was just a cover, wasn't it? You were actually searching for the nuggets. You'd checked all the other mines and found nothing and there was only one deserted mine left — the one on Mrs. Goodchild's ranch. Only you couldn't search there because it was on private property. So you tried to — "

Lion broke off abruptly. All resemblance to the friendly neighbour in unit fifteen had disappeared from Klein's face. The amusement in his eyes had changed to anger.

"I think we've chatted long enough." Klein's hand darted out. A second later, a length of thin nylon cord — identical to the cord tied across the trail yesterday — was wrapped around one of Lion's wrists.

"Lemme go!" Lion shouted, struggling to free himself. But Klein was too strong for him. The next minute, both hands were securely tied behind his back and he'd been dumped on his seat onto the hard ground. It didn't help that the sage brush he'd been thrown against was one of those particularly prickly ones Bobbi had complained about. He tried not to squirm. He didn't want to give Klein the satisfaction of knowing he was hurting, but the sharp prickles were needling right through his shirt.

"It's not easy to run fast with your hands tied," Klein said, looking down at Lion with amusement. "If you try it, I'll catch you and tie your feet as well. But don't worry. It won't be for long. I'll untie you when I put you down the shaft with your little friend."

Lion felt a smothering wave of panic. He'd been so busy working things out and thinking how dumb he'd been, he'd had no time to be scared. "You can't shut us down there," he protested, struggling frantically to free his hands.

The geologist's grin widened. "Of course I can. You've discovered far too much for me to let you go. But don't be frightened. It will be quite painless. I'm planning to use carbon monoxide. That's why I came back with my car. A hose attached to the exhaust pipe and leading down into the shaft, and in a few minutes both you and your little friend will go quietly to sleep." His smile widened. "She'll be glad to have you join her. I think it's nice to have company for something like that, don't you?"

The geologist enjoyed hurting people, Lion realized with increasing terror. "You'll never get away with it!" he managed to say through lips that were beginning to feel stiff and wooden.

The amusement in Klein's face grew. He sat down on the dry ground beside Lion and settled himself comfortably. "I think you're wrong about that. Yesterday after I saw your little friend racing home I guessed that she must have found the gold. So last night as soon as it was dark, I took the trouble to come out here and ready the mine shaft. It isn't hard to seal the air holes in an old shaft, you know, or to put down a small hose. It took hardly any time at all. Now it's just a question of fixing the other end of that hose to the exhaust pipe of my car." He seemed eager to boast to someone of his cleverness, even if it was only Lion.

Idly Klein brushed at some dirt on the knee of his jeans. "I was fully expecting her to slip out early this morning and come back to collect her treasure, so I was up and watching even earlier. When I saw her heading out, I followed. I let her climb back down the mine shaft entrance that you so cleverly discovered and get the nuggets. Why should I have risked going down into that shaky shaft if she would do it for me? When she came back out, I merely relieved her of her burden and convinced her to go back inside."

Klein was obviously enjoying the effect his words were having on his prisoner, for the self-satisfied smile grew broader. "I had expected to have only one underground guest, but two can be accommodated just as easily. Fifteen minutes — half an hour perhaps — and there will be no one to contradict my story that I was the one who found those nuggets, and that I found them in a mine shaft miles from here."

Lion was so scared it was hard to think clearly, but he realized his only hope was to keep Klein talking until Dad could get here. Only how? He squirmed to get away from the prickly sagebrush and tried to concentrate.

"Ouch!" The word was out before he could stop it. His fingers had hit a prickle so sharp he could feel the blood running.

Klein's grin widened. "Sagebrush is prickly, isn't it?"

But it hadn't been a sagebrush prickle that had cut his fingers, Lion realized. As he'd pushed down in the dirt behind his back in an effort to change his position, his hand had pressed against one of those pieces of broken beer bottle Bobbi had complained about. Would it be sharp enough to cut through the rope if he rubbed his bound wrists back and forth along the edge of the glass? He had to try.

"Did you steal that photograph because you were afraid it might show the mine entrance?" Lion asked. He already knew the answer, but it was the only question he could think to ask that might keep Klein talking a little longer.

The geologist smiled as Lion again grimaced in pain, then nodded. "That was one reason. I was afraid the angle at which you were shooting would give it away. I couldn't take the chance that you would show that photo to some gold seeker who might spot the hidden entrance, recognize the location, then help himself to those nuggets before I could find a way to get onto Mrs. Goodchild's property." Klein stopped talking. His eyes narrowed and he peered at Lion closely.

Lion froze. Did Klein suspect what he was doing? But the geologist couldn't have been suspicious after all. After a moment, the measuring look faded. He readjusted his position and continued to brag. "I've been pretty sure for almost a year now that this had to be where the nuggets were hidden."

Carefully, Lion again began sawing at the rope with the piece of broken bottle. He couldn't be sure how much of the rope was being cut, but he knew his wrists were. He could feel the blood warm and sticky on his fingers. "Is that why you pretended you wanted to buy property up here?" he asked, still trying to buy more sawing time. "So you'd have an excuse for hanging around?"

A glint of surprise crept into Klein's expression. "You found out about that, did you? Yes, I was hoping to get the Diamond A. But at the last minute that Goodchild woman changed her mind." Dislike and bitterness rang in his voice.

The caretaker must have been warning Mrs. Goodchild

about Klein in that conversation he'd overheard, Lion realized. She didn't trust Klein and knew he could be dangerous.

Lion continued to saw at the rope around his wrists. "What if Mrs. Goodchild had agreed to sell you her ranch, only the nuggets hadn't turned out to be worth as much as you'd had to pay out?"

"I didn't plan to pay anything. As soon as I'd collected my nuggets, I'd have found some way to cancel the deal. But that's enough talk." Klein got to his feet.

The ropes around Lion's wrists had loosened slightly. He was sure one of the strands had parted, but his hands were still held tight. He needed a little longer — "You said there was another reason why you wanted the photograph."

The gleam of amusement came back into Klein's eyes. "I realize of course that these questions are a delaying tactic, so this will be the last. The other reason I didn't want you to have that picture was so there'd be no concrete proof that Spud was here. Bea Goodchild had taken care that no one saw her niece or spoke to her. As a result I felt reasonably certain that the police would hesitate to start an official search for her. A picture, however, would have spoiled that." His eyes turned hard. "So, I'm afraid, has your interference here this morning."

Reaching into his pocket he pulled out a large ring of keys. He fingered through the keys until he found the one he wanted, then he looked again at Lion. "I'm fairly certain the police would not have searched for the girl, but they will search for you. So I will untie your hands just before I shut you down in the shaft. Then, after the carbon dioxide has done its work, I'll remove the hose and open the mine cover. That way it will look like an accident — nobody's fault, just two irresponsible kids exploring an old mine shaft without first making sure the underground gasses weren't deadly."

Another strand had loosened. Ignoring the cuts to his wrists, Lion again rubbed the rope hard against the broken bit of glass. This time he felt the final strand give. Keep still, he told himself urgently. He mustn't let Klein know he was free until he'd thought of some plan. Otherwise the geologist would just tie him up again.

"If you'll let us go," he began in a pleading voice, "we won't say anything. Honest!"

"I wonder how long you'd keep that promise!"

Lion let his shoulders slump, dropped his head and did his best to look scared and defeated. Maybe if Klein thought he'd given up, the geologist wouldn't watch him too closely.

It worked. Klein turned away. "You've delayed me long enough. It's time to get you settled." Pushing back a branch of the sagebrush, he fitted the key he was holding into one of the padlocks that anchored the steel bar across the wooden cover.

Frantically, Lion tried to think of something he could do. Then, for the first time since this whole thing had started, he remembered Rajah. He had an idea. But if it was going to work it had to be timed perfectly. He braced himself, and waited until he heard the tumblers in the padlock click open. Then he jumped to his feet. With fingers still numb from being tied so tightly, Lion grabbed the end of the branch of sage that the geologist had pushed out of the way. He pulled it back as far as it would reach, then let it go.

At the sound of Lion moving, the kneeling geologist had glanced back. The prickly branch was in a direct line with his face and shoulders. As it snapped back into place, it caught him a stinging blow.

"Damn you!" Klein cried, whirling around and reaching for Lion.

But Lion wasn't there. Even as the branch had snapped back, Lion was running. A dozen stumbling steps and he'd reached Rajah. Grabbing the reins so that the horse wouldn't think he was still ground tied, Lion flung them over Rajah's neck.

The geologist was almost upon him.

"Back him away, Rajah!" Lion shouted, dodging clear just as the geologist reached to grab him. "Dad said you were a cutting horse. Back him away and hold him."

It was like a freeze on TV. Lion didn't dare move in case it distracted Rajah. The horse and the geologist measured each other. If only Raj would understand, Lion breathed silently. What if he hadn't given the right command? Why hadn't he listened more carefully when Dad had been talking about cutting horses. Why hadn't he asked a few questions?

For a moment longer, Rajah watched the man facing him. Then he lowered his head. Slowly he began moving forward. The geologist backed up.

"Excellent!" Lion cheered excitedly. "Back him up farther, Rajah!"

The horse advanced another few steps, but this time the geologist was ready. Instead of moving back, he stooped, caught up a handful of dirt and pebbles and threw it in Rajah's face. Rajah jumped backward. The next moment, however, he was moving forward again, his head lowered, his eyes watching the man in front of him. Again Klein backed up. Now the geologist was half a dozen paces away from the mine entrance.

Was it far enough, Lion wondered? It had to be. He had to get that mine cover off. Spud might be running out of air. Leaving Rajah to look after the geologist, Lion ran back to the buried trap door.

The padlock on the right had been opened but the other was still clamped tight. That meant the metal rod which went through the ring was still anchored at one end. If he used a piece of rock to pry … But he had to be careful. If he jarred it too much …

Slowly the cover started to lift. One final push and it came free.

Quickly, Lion peered down. A wave of stale air met his

nostrils, then he saw a terrified white face staring up at him.

"I'll get you out! Just wait till I find something we can use as a ladder." The one that should have been there had obviously been taken away by the geologist. He looked around. If he could find a box, or a chunk of old timber that he could drop down for Spud to stand on, he could pull her out. He turned to check on Klein.

Rajah no longer had the geologist in check. Somewhere Klein had found a large two-by-four. It looked almost as grey and weathered as the wood of the mine cover, but it was still solid and heavy. Brandishing it in front of him, he moved toward the horse.

Eyeing the piece of wood, Rajah took a step backward.

The geologist lunged.

His timing was off. He missed the horse and hit empty air. The weight of the stick almost tore it from his grasp, and the end hit the ground with a sharp slap.

Again Rajah moved forward.

It was the geologist's turn to retreat, but this time, instead of moving straight back he moved sideways, toward where Lion was standing by the open mine shaft. Getting Spud out would have to wait, Lion realized. He could see what the geologist had in mind. Two more steps and Klein would be close enough to shove him into the open shaft with Spud and kick the wooden cover back in place. Then all the geologist would have to do was fight off the horse. "Move him back, Rajah!" Lion yelled. "Don't let him edge around in a circle. Keep him away from the mine entrance!"

Again Rajah moved forward, but this time Klein calculated the distance between them more successfully. He timed his lunge so that the heavy stick didn't swing into empty air but struck Rajah's shoulder with a stinging blow.

The horse grunted in pain. He stared at the geologist in confusion. Before he could decide what to do, Klein hit him again.

Rajah looked even more confused. He took a step backward. Then his head lowered.

It was okay, Lion saw with relief. He was going to move forward again.

But at that very moment Rajah paused. His head lifted. He turned slightly in the direction of the road, listening.

Lion heard it, too. So did the geologist. It was a car motor. "It'll be Dad and Bobbi, Rajah! Hold him just a couple more minutes," Lion called excitedly.

But Rajah was moving away.

"Come back you dumb horse!" Lion shouted. "Do your job! Hold him!"

But it seemed Rajah wasn't interested in playing hero any longer.

The next moment, Dad's station wagon slid to a stop on the dry prairie grass next to the red Camaro. Dad burst out of one front door and Bobbi tumbled out of the other. Another car came racing toward them — the one Lion had glimpsed over top of that hillock a while earlier. It too slid to a halt. Riley got out of the driver's side while a shaken, white-faced Mrs. Goodchild climbed out of the passenger seat, followed by an ecstatic black-and-white dog.

A moment later, a third car topped the rise. This time it was an R.C.M.P. patrol car with a uniformed police officer behind the wheel.

25

Everyone started speaking at once.

"I'll ask you to come with me, sir," the policeman said to the stunned geologist.

"I was so scared!" Spud confessed in a shaking voice as Dad and Riley pulled her up from the shaft, and her aunt folded her in her arms.

"Thank goodness you're safe! Thank goodness you're safe!" Mrs. Goodchild said over and over in a voice that was little more than a hoarse whisper.

"I would have told you last night, but I wanted to surprise you," Spud said against her aunt's shoulder. "Dad said the nuggets belonged to you and that those other people were trying to steal them from you. He said he was going to find them, then surprise you by having them waiting on the table when you came in." She gulped back her sobs. "That's what I was trying to do —"

Mrs. Goodchild hugged her tighter.

"Didn't you know how dangerous it was," Riley scolded gently, "coming out here to collect something worth that much money without somebody to look after you?" He might as well not have spoken, for Spud continued to hug her aunt as if she'd never let her go, and both of them were crying.

Lion stood beside Bobbi watching the others with a delighted grin. He rubbed his sore wrists.

"I bet those hurt," Bobbi said quietly.

"A bit."

"Tell me again what happened."

Before Lion could repeat his story, Spud released her aunt. She brushed a hand across her eyes, leaving a muddy smear on one cheek, and moved toward them. "I was so scared," she told Lion shyly. "But when I heard you keeping that man talking and talking I knew you had a plan, so I wasn't so scared any more." She smiled at him.

Lion felt his cheeks flush fiery red. Being made to feel like a hero wasn't the sort of thing that happened to him every day. To be honest, being made to feel like a hero wasn't the sort of thing that happened to him any day. Especially not by a girl.

"Hey, it was nothing," he managed, feeling even more embarrassed as he realized that both Dad and Bobbi were watching. But Spud might think he was a nerd if he couldn't say more than that, so in a rush he added, "We saw your witching rod in that room in the barn. Can you really find stuff with that thing?"

Spud's smile deepened. "If you want, I'll show you how it works sometime."

Lion blushed even harder.

"In the meantime," Dad said, moving closer, "I'm curious to know how you and your sister define the word 'dangerous.' Somehow or other I had the silly idea that for the duration of this trip you had agreed to restrict your activities to harmless sightseeing."

"We didn't think it'd be dangerous," Lion defended himself.

Dad's eyes lifted skyward in mute appeal. "How can a mere parent fight against twelve-year-old logic," he said to no one in particular.

Lion wasn't fooled. In a minute Dad would recover, and when he did, rules might be made. Before that could happen he said brightly, "There's something I still don't understand. If Spud wasn't being locked in the barn, why did she need to use the secret exit that first night?"

"Riley told her to leave that way," Dad replied. "He knew you and Bobbi were hiding in the stall and he didn't want you to see her."

"He knew we were there? We didn't fool him?" Lion's self-esteem plummeted. He didn't want to be a secret agent after all, he decided. Space pilot would be way better.

"Since I'm well aware," Dad went on wryly, "that the reason for that question was to make me forget about your promise to stay out of trouble, is there anything else you'd like to ask?"

Lion grinned self-consciously. When would he learn it was useless trying to con Dad?

"If you ever catch me even thinking about getting on a horse again," Lion remarked the following afternoon as they finished loading the horses into the horse trailer, "shoot me. Every spot that isn't blistered is aching."

"You'll have forgotten your aches and pains by tomorrow, and by the next day the blisters will have turned into calluses." Bobbi swung her saddle and bridle up onto the saddle tree at the back of the trailer and moved out of the way so Lion could do the same with his.

"No, they won't, because I'm never riding again." He put away his tack then glared at Rajah, who, like Brie, was leisurely munching the hay Bobbi had put in the feed box at the front of the trailer. "Particularly not on that stupid animal."

Bobbi tried not to smile. "I don't call what he did stupid. I call it pretty darn smart."

"To walk off and leave me?"

"He knew the war was won by then, and he was opting for non-violence."

"You mean opting to save his own hide. Some cutting horse. No wonder they sold him to us. At the first sign of trouble he forgets what he's been trained to do."

"Not exactly the first sign of trouble," Bobbi said, her eyes brimming with laughter. "You told us Otto Klein gave him a couple of pretty good whacks with that two-by-four."

Lion grinned. "That's true. He did. But that's no reason for the dumb horse to desert me."

"Maybe he knew it was okay to go by then. Horses recognize car motors the way dogs do, you know."

"Come on! There's no way he could have known that was Dad's car."

"Yes, there is. He'd driven behind it all the way from Vancouver."

"He took off before we even heard the car coming."

"Before you did, but maybe not before he did."

Lion continued to scowl, but Bobbi's words had started him thinking. He moved back into the trailer, pushed past Brie and drew even with Rajah's head.

Rajah looked up from his feed box.

"Did you recognize the car?" Lion asked, staring the horse in the face. "Did you know it was Dad? Was that why you left? Or had you decided you'd had enough of that stick and wanted to save your own hide?"

For a long moment Rajah returned Lion's look. Then he put his head back down in the hay.

"Stupid horse! The trouble is, how will I ever know?"

Bobbi burst out laughing.

At that moment Dad emerged from the motel. "That's it. I think we can be on our way."

It had been a busy morning. Dad had taken Mrs. Goodchild into Quesnel to meet with the Ministry people and she'd been granted permanent guardianship rights. The bag of nuggets had been found hidden under several blankets in the trunk of Otto Klein's red Camaro, and was now locked in a safe in the appraiser's office. Bobbi and Lion, with Dad in attendance, had given sworn statements to the police about what had happened at the mine site, and the geologist was a permanent guest in the police station. Now they could go home.

Together Bobbi and Lion raised the trailer ramp and fastened it firmly in place, then moved toward the station wagon.

"D'you want the front seat this time?" Bobbi asked.

Lion grinned and shook his head. "The back's fine."

For the first few kilometres no one spoke. Then Lion sat forward as far as the seat belt would allow. "What happens to Spud's family ranch?" he asked.

"The ranch is Spud's. For the next few years she'll live with her aunt, and the ranch will be managed by the foreman and his wife. But it will belong to her, and as soon as she's old enough, she will take over."

"Does the gold go to Mrs. Goodchild?"

"Yes, because it was found on her property."

Lion digested that for a minute. "So what's she gonna do with all that money?"

"Put in some irrigation on her ranch, if she's smart," Dad replied.

"And refurbish the guest room," Bobbi said with a saucy grin.

Dad glanced sideways. "Has she invited you for a visit?"

Bobbi's smile broadened. "She has invited both Lion and

me. She's going to phone you in a few days and make the arrangements. She said something about Spud wanting to teach Lion to witch."

For a moment something outside the window required Lion's attention and he missed the look that passed between his sister and his dad.

Again there was silence. Then Dad said innocently, "What about Rajah?"

Lion looked up to find Dad watching him through the rearview mirror. The question caught him off guard. In his mind, he'd been busy practising witching. "How d'you mean, what about him?"

"From some of the things you've said, I rather suspect that you and Rajah might not be on the best of terms. If you want to be rid of him I'll see what I can do about finding another owner."

For a moment Lion's seat belt required adjusting. Then, at his coolest and most worldly, he said, "How can we stick somebody else with a horse as dumb as he is? Think how guilty we'd feel."

"Then you want to keep him?"

"There's nothing else we can do."

Neither Dad nor Bobbi spoke, but this time Lion caught the look that passed between them. Again they drove for a few minutes in silence. Then Dad said quietly, "I trust this won't be misinterpreted as an invitation for you to plunge headlong into any more of my cases, but in this instance I'm glad you two came along."

"I knew you'd need us," Lion said delightedly.

Dad's eyebrows lifted. "I don't want to sound ungrateful, but please don't feel you have to repeat this performance."

Lion grinned. "So where do we go next, Dad?"

"I thought you were opposed to family togetherness and mosquitoes and outdoor plumbing."

"I've changed my mind." Lion looked back out the window

and tried to sound twelve and three-quarters. "This has been kind of neat."

Dad's surprised glance was reflected in the rear-view mirror. But when he spoke there was no evidence of anything but normal interest in his voice. "Sometime next week I've promised to drive up the Sunshine Coast to the Powell River area," he said matter-of-factly.

Lion abandoned the window. "To see a client?"

"A friend, actually. But with a possible legal problem."

"What sort of problem?"

"I know what you're thinking, and forget it. But it's interesting country. If you and Bobbi want to come along we could take the horses and —"

Lion forgot about looking cool and worldly. He even forgot about trying to look twelve-and-three-quarters. Leaning as far forward as the seat belt would allow, he tucked his head over the front seat. "You want to, Bobbi?"

"If you do."

Lion settled back against the cushions. "Hey, excellent," he said.

Joan Weir is a widely published writer for young readers. Her numerous books include *Sixteen is Spelled O-U-C-H* (Stoddart), *Mystery at Lighthouse Rock* (Stoddart), and *Ski Lodge Mystery* (Stoddart). She is a creative writing instructor at the University College of the Cariboo. Joan Weir lives — and rides her horse Raj (the model for Lion's horse) — in Kamloops, British Columbia.